HER SWEET CARESS

Her laughter faded when he grasped her fingers with his left hand. As he had guessed, she did not dare to tug away, fearing that not only would she cause him to shower himself with soup, but that her action might injure his wounded arm. Taking the cup from him, she stretched to place it on the table when he did not release her fingers.

"I am sorry, Miss Dunsworthy, for anything boorish that I said and did that night," he said in barely more than a whisper. "I can assure you that if I had been myself, as you put it so generously, I would have cut off my left arm before I would have hurt you."

"I know that." Her voice was as hushed as his, each word slipping along him like a cat's purring caress.

"Lucian."

"What?"

"Call me Lucian, and grant me the privilege of calling you Bianca."

<u>BOOK YOUR PLACE ON OUR WEBSITE</u>
<u>AND MAKE THE</u>
<u>READING CONNECTION!</u>

We've created a customized website just for our very special readers, where you can get the inside scoop on everything that's going on with Zebra, Pinnacle and Kensington books.

When you come online, you'll have the exciting opportunity to:

- View covers of upcoming books
- Read sample chapters
- Learn about our future publishing schedule (listed by publication month *and author*)
- Find out when your favorite authors will be visiting a city near you
- Search for and order backlist books from our online catalog
- Check out author bios and background information
- Send e-mail to your favorite authors
- Meet the Kensington staff online
- Join us in weekly chats with authors, readers and other guests
- Get writing guidelines
- AND MUCH MORE!

Visit our website at
http://www.kensingtonbooks.com

The Perfect Bride

Jo Ann Ferguson

ZEBRA BOOKS

KENSINGTON PUBLISHING CORP.

http://www.kensingtonbooks.com

ZEBRA BOOKS are published by

Kensington Publishing Corp.
850 Third Avenue
New York, NY 10022

All Kensington titles, imprints and distributed lines are available at special quantity discounts for bulk purchases for sales promotion, premiums, fund-raising, educational or institutional use.

Special book excerpts or customized printings can also be created to fit specific needs. For details, write or phone the office of the Kensington Special Sales Manager: Kensington Publishing Corp., 850 Third Avenue, New York, NY 10022. Attn. Special Sales Department. Phone: 1-800-221-2647.

First Printing: October 2004
10 9 8 7 6 5 4 3 2 1

Printed in the United States of America

For Bill,
my *perfect match*

PROLOGUE

Most people walked right past the carving on the church wall. Some stopped to look at the parade of saints walking widdershins along the church, as if tempting the fairy folk to appear. Yet, even those who did slow failed to pause long enough to read the inscription beneath the stone saints' feet.

Covered with moss and almost lost among the twisting vines of climbing roses, the words remained a curse and a blessing:

Once, twice, thrice—
Be it by heaven or by the devil's own device
What joy or grief for one shall be worthy
Shall come the same for each Dunsworthy

Chapter One

"I will see you for grass before breakfast!"

Lucian Wandersee, fourth earl of that title, tossed his cards onto the table and stood. "I think not, Andover."

"You have insulted me by—"

"I have neither insulted you nor have I done anything to change Lady Rockington's affections toward you. If the lady has decided that her heart is going to lead her elsewhere, then that has been by her decision alone. Or, at least, without my involvement." He pulled on his dark coat and downed the last of the wine in his glass before glaring at Andover, who with his bright red hair and furious scowl resembled a puffed-up rooster. "By all that's blue, Andover, I give you my word as a gentleman that I have not spoken more than a score of words to the lady."

"As a gentleman?" Andover drew himself up to his full height, which was still half a head shorter than Lucian's. "That is a jest. No gentleman would—"

Lucian drove his fist into the shorter man's nose and watched the baron collapse into a chair, knocking it and himself to the floor. Looking at the other men listening with impatience, for they were eager to return to their cards and conversation, he arched a dark brow. "Mayhap no gentleman would, but I was quite happy to."

Another man stood. "Pay him no mind, Wandersee. You tolerated his prattle longer than I would have. Come back to the table while good fortune is with us."

"Good fortune is with *you,* Carlson. Not me." He pocketed the handful of coins left in front of where he had been sitting.

Stepping over Andover, whose hushed groans warned that he soon would be regaining his senses, Lucian walked from the room. He looked in both directions along the upper gallery of the club that he had been mad to become a member of only five years ago. Obtaining membership had offered him a challenge, and he enjoyed a challenge. Then and now.

But in the wake of his service on the Continent in the war against that blasted Corsican, playing cards and giving a bottle a black eye seemed less than challenging. To own the truth, doing that night after night was boring. He had never thought he would find London filling him with *ennui,* but he was.

"Wandersee!"

Lucian turned to see Franklin Bullock motioning to him from the other side of the gallery that ringed the stairs leading down to the ground floor. Knowing Bullock would not believe that Lucian had not taken note of him, Lucian waited for the man, who was built like the beast that had inspired his family's name, to lumber around the gallery to where Lucian was standing.

"Glad I could catch you before you took your leave," Bullock said, huffing as if he had run from Hyde Park. "You may want to avoid Andover today."

"Too late. I just spoke with him." He rubbed his knuckles which still stung from the concussion against the baron's nose.

"If you need a second—"

"I have no need for a second, because there will be no duel." He leaned one elbow on the cast-iron railing between the thick pillars. "I refused Andover's challenge."

"Refused? But you cannot do that!"

"I did."

Bullock scratched his chin, where dark whiskers indicated he had not been home to enjoy the attentions of his valet in more than a day. "Andover will be livid."

"Mayhap when he wakes." He tapped the reddened knuckles of his right hand.

With a laugh, Bullock said, "He has been bragging for almost a week that he would make you rue your dalliance with Rockington's wife."

"I leave chasing after the skirts of another man's wife to Andover and his ilk. I have no interest in any wife."

"Even your own?"

"Do not sound like a matchmaking mother. It does not suit you."

Again Bullock laughed. "If you heeded *on dits*, Wandersee, you would know that I am only asking to your face what others whisper behind your back. Everyone is eager to discover when the earl is going to select a bride. It is rumored that Lydia Meyers is the one upon whom you have set your cap."

"Lydia asked me to escort her and her grandmother to the theater one evening when Sellman was ill. 'Twas a favor for a longtime friend, nothing more."

He laughed wryly and shook his head. "I would have guessed that the *ton* had better things to do than worry about my matrimonial state."

"The Season is over, and those who linger in Town are seeking any sort of entertainment."

Lucian pushed himself away from the railing. "I have no interest in providing it for them. Mayhap it is time for me to take my leave as well." He grimaced. "Wandersee Manor is still being renovated, and I have no interest in getting involved in my mother's plans for the house."

Bullock chuckled as they walked down the stairs. "I knew you to be a wise man, Wandersee. You are welcome to join me at my dirty acres."

"All the way in the north of England? I appreciate the offer, Bullock, but I have to be in Bath for Jordan's wedding in late September. I do not fancy the idea of riding the length of England twice in such a short time."

"Which Jordan? The viscount or his younger brother?" He tapped his chin. "What are the lads' names?"

"Rupert is the viscount, and his title is Fortenbury now that he has inherited from his uncle. 'Tis Henry who is being wed."

"Ah, yes, I forgot Henry Jordan had decided to marry Wallace's younger daughter." He laughed again. "September, is it? I guess he wishes to take no chance on her returning here for the Season and having another chap catch her eye."

"I suspect Henry grew tired of listening to his mother remind him of the need for an heir as his bookish brother has yet to consider a bride. However, he seems quite enamored with the young woman, singing her praises until my ears are quite overfull. He has arranged for a gathering in a few weeks at his house near Plymouth. I would guess he is eager to take a break from the wedding plans at the family's estate in Bath, although his betrothed is to be at this gathering."

"It sounds rather as if he is starting the celebration early."

"Celebrating about to be leg-shackled? I would say it is more likely he intends to have the company of his fellow bachelors this one final time, and he knows that the only way to do so is to have a party to which feminine guests are invited to keep his fiancée occupied."

Bullock clapped him on the back as they reached the ground floor. "One of these days, you will find yourself thinking relentlessly of a pair of flashing eyes and beguiling curves. After all, you have a duty to your title, too. Has no woman intrigued you enough to consider buckling yourself to her?"

"Now you *are* sounding like a matchmaker. Leave off. When the time comes, I suspect the lady will make herself quite clear in her intentions, so I can be equally forthright in mine."

"Is that what you think?" Bullock put his hands on his massive belly as he roared with laughter. In the galley above, two footmen stopped and peered over the railing to see what was happening below. "Ladies are seldom as obvious as a man would hope. Mayhap it is because we have become accustomed to the candid behavior of our convenients. Do you agree?"

Lucian considered his possible answers with care. If he spoke of how he had not bothered with a pursuit in that direction either since his return to England,

Bullock would label him a beef-head and worse. Saying that his mind was scattered and that he was having trouble regaining the easy bachelor's fare that he had enjoyed before his commission took him to the Continent might bring more ridicule from Bullock, who had lambasted him as an air-dreamer for buying that captaincy in the first place. Nor would Bullock understand if Lucian were to relate that he was tired of the posturing of petty fools like Andover when he had become familiar with the straightforward ways of soldiers who knew pride could be fatal.

Better to change the subject, so he did. He began to speak of politics, a favorite topic for Bullock, as they opened the door, letting the bustle of St. James's Street invade the club's hush. Walking down the steps to the narrow street, Lucian drew on his gloves while Bullock spoke to the footman by the door, asking for their carriages to be brought.

A hint of a mist was weighing down the air. Narrow fingers of fog were already crawling along the street, and Lucian guessed the fog and smoke from the chimney pots would be thick tonight.

"So you are going?" Bullock asked.

Lucian knew he had let his attention wander too far because he had not heard anything else Bullock had said since they emerged from the club. "Going where?"

"Jordan's seaside gathering."

"I had thought that one round of toasts to the happy couple would be enough, so I plan only to attend the wedding."

"That is a shame. You shall miss the sight in Plymouth Harbor."

"Sight?"

"It is said that the *H.M.S. Bellerophon* and its imperial passenger will be bound there to await the orders to transfer Napoleon to another ship for his final exile on St. Helena."

Lucian's mouth tightened. He was infuriated that after so many men on both sides had died for wars fought solely to obtain the Corsican an empire throughout Europe, that Napoleon was being treated like a respected prisoner. "A waste of time and manpower," he growled.

"These things must be handled with care," Bullock said, stepping back as a passing carriage splattered water onto the walkway. "He did put himself in English hands."

"To escape the Russians who would have dealt with him quickly and efficiently."

"But he is our problem now, and the laws of England must outweigh the yearning for vengeance."

"That is your opinion."

"Yes."

"It is not mine." He smiled coldly as his carriage came into view. "Banishing Napoleon yet again is a disgrace. How can we let him go unchallenged for the deeds he has done? A man must be made to pay for his wrongs."

An icy laugh came from behind him, and something sharp cut into his spine. Looking back, he saw Andover and a man he knew only by sight as a member of the club.

"I am glad to hear you say that, Wandersee," Andover crowed, "because I feel the same way. You have wronged me, and I demand satisfaction."

Lucian started to turn, but Bullock's abruptly pale face warned him to take due caution. Stretching his neck to an awkward angle, he saw that the sharp finger in his back was the long barrel of a pistol. He cursed silently. Andover was foxed, so foxed he might fire the gun by mistake.

"I have told you, Andover, that I will not accept your challenge." He hoped his calm voice would reach through the man's drunken haze.

"You have wronged me!" He screeched the words so loudly that all along the street people stopped to stare. "I demand satisfaction."

"You shall not have it from me."

"Then I shall kill you where you stand!"

Bullock choked, "By the elevens, Wandersee, humor the man. Accept his challenge."

"No." Lucian crossed his arms over his chest, but doubted he betwattled anyone with this careless pose. Acting out of hand now could mean Andover shooting him where he stood. Mayhap if he kept this conversation going long enough, someone would wrest the gun from Andover's hand. He had little hope of that, because in the scuffle the gun could easily be fired.

"Do not be a fool, Wandersee!" cried Bullock, his face turning a dangerous shade of gray-green. When the man wobbled, the footman hesitated only a moment, then ran to steady him.

Lucian took a single step toward his friend, but the pistol in his back was a silent warning to remain where he was.

"Andover," Lucian said, keeping his voice calm, "you have distressed Bullock so with your antics that the man is taking ill."

" 'Tis not his state of health that should concern

you, but your own." Andover emphasized his words by pressing the gun more deeply into Lucian's back.

A groan from Bullock, who was leaning heavily on the footman as both sank toward the walkway, warned that the man might be worse than ill. He watched the footman lower Bullock onto his back and loosen his collar. This could not be allowed to go on any longer.

"If I accept your unwarranted challenge, will you let this be done with for now?"

"I would gladly have this done with now."

Lucian frowned. He could not mistake the drunken tremor in Andover's voice. Agreeing would put an end to this farce on St. James's Street, and surely Andover would come to his senses when he was no longer in his cups.

"Very well," he said. "I accept your accursed challenge." The gun remained at his back. "Deuce take it, Andover! I have accepted your dashed challenge. Now let me go and see if Bullock needs help."

"The footman can take care of that. I want my satisfaction now."

"Now?" He wanted to turn and demand if Andover was completely mad, but he knew that might be the very action to guarantee Andover firing the gun. "At this hour, there are ladies and children at any of the areas commonly used as dueling greens in Hyde Park or Green Park."

"Then we shall face each other here."

"Here? You may have forgotten, Andover, but dueling is not authorized by law. Certainly it is not allowed on St. James's Street. The watch will be here before a single shot is fired."

Andover chuckled with malevolent glee. "You need

not worry about that, Wandersee. You shall not be alive to witness that. Or have you forgotten how often I bested you in shooting when we were younger?"

He had not forgotten. Andover was a skilled marksman, far more so than Lucian could ever aspire to be. If Andover were not as drunk as a piper, Lucian would remind the baron that Lucian had served on the Continent. That might have given Andover pause, even though Lucian had not fired his gun often during his time there.

The pistol jabbed in his back, and he was bumped forward a step. He looked over his shoulder. Andover was handing the pistol to his companion, whom he addressed as Markham. At the same time, Andover was raising his hand to reveal another pistol. People drew back in horror, edging into doorways and calling desperately for the watch as Lucian was herded to the middle of the narrow street. Andover walked the width of five buildings from him and raised the pistol.

"This should be about the twenty paces we should have between us," Andover bellowed. When a man moved toward him, pleading with Andover to rethink this madness, Andover shifted the gun, and the man froze before inching back onto the walkway.

Shouts came from the clubs and the shops on either side of the street, but Lucian ignored them as Markham withdrew the gun from his back and shoved it into his hand. A quick check told him it was primed and ready to be fired. His thought to grab Markham and use him as a hostage to persuade Andover to be sensible was an idea he tossed aside. Andover was in such a pelter, he might shoot his own second.

Glancing at the walkway in front of the club, Lucian saw that Bullock was being helped to his feet and away from where a wild shot might strike him. His face was no longer the pasty color of death, but his eyes were so wide that Lucian feared they would roll right out of his head.

"Wandersee!"

At Andover's shout, Lucian hefted the pistol. He wished he could think of a way to put an end to this without further hullabaloo. He could not.

"On the count of three, Wandersee!"

He saw people scrambling for cover and heard more shouts as bets were called out as it was wagered which one of them would be the victor in this outrageous duel in the middle of St. James's. He held his pistol at the ready as Andover smiled and slowly began the count. The baron was so drunk that he was acting as if this were sport.

"Three!" Andover shouted and fired. The detonation seemed unbelievably loud on the street.

Pain burst along Lucian's left arm. He looked down to see blood pooling on his best coat's sleeve. That Andover had ruined his favorite coat vexed him for the second before pain gushed through him, rocking him backward. He fought to maintain his footing and raised his head. Andover was staring at him, looking abruptly sober as he realized the enormity of what he had done.

Knowing he should fire either at Andover or up into the air, Lucian walked to the walkway and handed the gun to the footman who had assisted Bullock to his feet. Lucian would not take the chance of the ball striking someone watching from an upper floor.

His coachee, Moss, rushed forward and pulled Lucian's right arm onto his shoulder. Lucian leaned against him as voices came at him from all directions. He heeded none of them while his ears rang as if they were bells being struck again and again.

"Yes," he replied to Moss's question if he could drive Lucian home.

Andover rushed up, chattering like an Indian monkey. Through the cacophony in his ears, Lucian heard him say, "But the duel is not over until both men have fired."

"You want me to shoot you?" Lucian asked, struggling to form each word.

"My honor remains unredeemed."

" 'Tis your good fortune that it is not your corpse that must be salvaged," he growled as he turned toward his carriage. Andover must be just as much of a widgeon when he was sober as when he was drunk.

"You cannot leave yet!" Andover grasped his bloody sleeve.

Pain seared through him, and the reaction was instinctive, but not unsatisfactory as Lucian's fist hit Andover's face squarely again. The baron struck the stone walkway hard, senseless once more.

Bullock stepped forward as the coachman helped Lucian into the carriage. Sitting on the comfortable seat, Lucian grimaced when he saw the blood still flowing down his arm. Bullock pulled off his own coat and handed it to him.

"No need, sir," Moss said. The coachman pulled some rags from the boot and handed them to Lucian. "I keep these around for polishing the carriage. They should work well, my lord."

"Thank you, Moss." He forced a smile for his

friend and the others watching. "And thank you, Bullock."

"Have that wound checked so it does not fester," Bullock ordered. "Then rest." He smiled suddenly. "Go to Jordan's party and let the sea air help heal you. Watching Napoleon sail away would do you good now."

"That is an excellent idea." He motioned for the tiger to close the door.

"I will see you there." Bullock raised his hand to wave.

Lucian leaned his head back against the seat. Leaving London now seemed like the best idea anyone had suggested in a very long time. There was an undeniable pleasure in anticipating being witness to Napoleon's banishment to the nether regions of the Atlantic. Traveling to Plymouth across the breadth of England would be a challenge for a man just shot in a duel in the middle of St. James's. It was not a challenge he would have wished for, but it was one he would take.

Chapter Two

"I swear that the wind is about to blow the roof right off!"

Bianca Dunsworthy chuckled at her sister's fearful gasp, which had interrupted the story she was reading aloud. Aiming a wary glance at the ceiling, she hoped Rosie was not prophetic. This summer storm seemed determined to do to the cottage's thatched roof what the winter had not. Thunder thudded almost overhead in the wake of eye-blurring lightning, and wind whistled under the eaves. By her side, the lamp's flames faltered before rallying.

"Do you wish me to go on, Rosie?" she asked, using her sister's nickname, because her sister despised her real name of Primrose. Bianca thought it fit her because her sister was always sunny and lovely to have nearby, but she knew the quickest way to vex her sister was to call her by her given name.

Rosie wrapped her arms around herself and nodded. "Just make sure the hero does not set sail in a storm like this one. I fear he would not survive to reach the end of the tale." She rose and went to the parlor window, which offered a view of the sea through the trees. "I do hate the waves when they become so loud and high."

"They are not high enough to reach Dunsworthy Dower Cottage." Bianca closed the book on her lap. "Do you think that whichever Lord Dunsworthy built this house wanted his own mother to come to harm after she retired here?"

"Mayhap he hoped she would wash out to sea."

Bianca laughed again. Rosie's russet hair refused to stay properly beneath her cap, but her younger sister was so lovely that she caught the eye of every passing man. Not that Rosie was a coquette. Quite the opposite, for Rosie was so shy she would not say boo to a goose. She would stop singing—a pastime that gave her the greatest joy—if anyone chanced to hear her. Bianca had never been described as reticent, and she doubted she could ever aspire to being as sweet as her sister. Words refused to go unsaid once they formed on her tongue.

She bent and scooped up one of the pair of cats wandering about the room and settled the tabby on her lap. Not only would Tabby's purr help drown out the thunder, but she could keep the cat from turning a hungry eye toward the box of chicks set on the low, stone hearth. She had brought them in when storm clouds had gathered on the horizon, and the wind had begun its fitful moan. During the last storm, the hens had cached their chicks in every possible hiding place around the hedgerow, and it had taken her and Rosie and Aunt Millicent three days to find them all. Two of the chicks had not survived, and they did not want to have others die in this storm.

"It shall be no sailing on the high sea for our hero," Bianca said, shifting on the low stool. "Come and sit, Rosie. The story shall take place when there is not a storm cloud in the sky."

"Are you telling us a story or reading us one this evening?" Aunt Millicent asked as she walked into the sitting room with a tray holding three glasses of lemonade. It would be the perfect drink, for the air in the small house was very close. Only a decade older than Bianca, for she was Bianca's father's youngest sister, she had hair a gold that seldom was found beyond fairy tales. Sitting beside where Rosie perched on the settee with the other cat in her lap, she added, "Your stories are far better than any in that book, Bianca."

"Yes, do give us one from your own imagination!" seconded Rosie. "Tell the one about the fancy ball and the masked rogue who lured that lovely young woman to her ruin in the white garden."

"Primrose Dunsworthy, you should not speak so!"

At her aunt's scold, Bianca laughed. "Aunt Millicent, she is hoaxing you. You know my stories are always appropriate for my sister's ears." She fired a frown at Rosie. She had not thought her sister would mention *that* tale when Aunt Millicent was in earshot, for it was no fiction but the sad story oft-repeated at Mrs. Hanover's store in the village as a warning to all young misses.

"Apparently others are not so circumspect." Aunt Millicent's smile returned as she wiped off the bottom of a glass so it would not drip on the cat, and handed it to Bianca. "However, the story of a glorious gathering on a lovely, starlit evening would be a nice counterpoint to this stormy night."

Taking a sip of the overly sweet lemonade, Bianca set the book on the table beside her. Tabby was now asleep on her lap, so she wrapped her arms around the cat and her knees as she began. "The earl's house is aglow in anticipation of the gathering to come. Every window, and you know there are dozens, glitter with candlelight. All along the long drive, lanterns are strung, so every lady who arrives in her grand carriage shines with gold and gems from the moment she rides onto the earl's lands. Music, like angels singing of love and glory, slips from the house to swirl beneath the trees like a country dance. When—" She turned as something crashed outside. Had a tree struck the house?

Aunt Millicent hurried to the window with her dog Barley close on her heels. The bushy brown-and-white dog was half the size of a horse, but somehow he managed to get through the parlor, with its trio of chairs and a settee and tables, without striking one.

With a relieved sigh, Aunt Millicent said, " 'Twas just a branch striking the front of the house, I suspect, because I do not see any trees down in the yard."

The cat hissed at Barley and jumped off Bianca's lap. The dog ignored Tabby.

"Do you want me to go out on the porch and check?" Bianca asked.

"Oh, no!" cried Rosie, coming to her feet. "You could be hurt! Another branch might come loose and strike you."

"You fret too much."

Aunt Millicent smiled and patted Bianca's shoulder before sitting again and motioning for Rosie to do the same. "Let's enjoy our lemonade and wait for the storm to pass. There will be time enough after the storm to explore and see what damage has been done. I hope the wind does not pluck more shingles from the barn roof. There are enough leaks already."

"Yes," seconded Rosie. "Do continue your story,

Bianca, so we can ignore the storm." She pushed Barley's nose away from the cat on her lap. It was arching its back, not to hiss, but to rub up against the dog. "I love to hear about such grand parties. If only we could go to London for the Season and see one for ourselves."

Aunt Millicent frowned, and Bianca wished her sister would remember to think before she spoke about the one subject that made them all uncomfortable. A fancy Season in London was not in their futures. Their father had been a baron, but because of his love of gambling he had died without two shillings to pinch together. Their mother had been the daughter of a country squire. So many times before she died, Lady Dunsworthy had thrilled a much younger Bianca with stories of the splendid parties that she had enjoyed with their father in London. Bianca had shared those stories with her younger sister.

Bianca closed her eyes and sighed. What Mama had spoken of would never be part of their lives. After Mama and Papa had died from an illness that swept over the shire, leaving so many dead in its wake, she and Rosie and their older brother Kevin had been left in the care of Aunt Millicent who came to live with them. Rosie had been little more than a baby, but Bianca recalled the sobs ringing through Dunsworthy Hall and the funeral, where she was first introduced to Aunt Millicent.

Dear Aunt Millicent had set aside her plans for her own Season to take care of three young orphans. They had lived in Dunsworthy Hall for many years, happy and content, although never with any extravagance. Then Kevin had come into an unexpected legacy from an uncle and had used the money to buy a commission and go in search of adventure. He joined several friends to fight in the battles against the French. None of them had returned, and the title and Dunsworthy Hall, on the far side of the hill behind the rose-covered cottage, went to a cousin none of them had ever met.

Without Aunt Millicent, who had brought Bianca and Rosie to live with her in this comfortable cottage that had been left to her by her father, Bianca wondered what she and her sister would have done after Kevin's death. It had been almost two years since the word had arrived at Dunsworthy Hall of his death, but the grief remained fresh.

"Such farradiddles are not a bad way to pass a stormy night," her aunt said, drawing Bianca's attention back to the present, "but you must remember that Bianca's stories are just farradiddles."

"And we have excitement right here close to home. Remember that there will be dancing and singing at the church festival that is coming soon," Bianca added, wanting to bring the bright glow back into her sister's green eyes. "If—"

The dog whined lowly, interrupting her. Bianca glanced at Barley. He was staring at the door, which she could see through the arch opening onto the foyer, his tail between his legs and his mouth drawn back in a growl.

"He probably is bothered by the wind," Rosie whispered, all the humor gone from her voice.

"Mayhap." Bianca hurried to the door. Opening it, she stared at the rain swirling through the trees that hid the road and the gray line of the sea. She could hear waves crashing furiously on the shore, but saw nothing out of the ordinary.

She started to close the door, but Barley pushed forward. He faced the sea, his nose twitching.

"Barley, 'tis too stormy to chase rabbits tonight," she chided.

He glanced at her with a rather disgusted expression, then rushed out onto the front steps. His tail wagged once, then drooped as he stood as straight as a soldier.

Bianca peered again through the storm, not sure what she was looking for. Whatever bothered the dog was something she could not see.

"Close the door and come back inside!" called Rosie as lightning darted through the sky. "If Barley wants to go out, let him go."

"Barley!" Bianca called.

He turned and bounced back into the house, now regarding her as if he could not understand why she was still standing by the door.

She closed it, then gasped as she heard a steady rapping. *That* was not a branch striking the house, for the sound came from knuckles against the door. Who was out on such a horrendous night? Glancing toward the parlor, she saw Rosie and Aunt Millicent coming to their feet. Incredulity widened their eyes. Was it this caller who had alerted Barley?

"Don't answer it!" cried Rosie, then pressed her hands over her mouth.

"If it is some lost soul—"

"More likely a renegade eager to prey on three women! No one else would be foolish enough to be out in this storm."

Bianca squared her shoulders. "Do not be silly. You have listened to too many of my stories, and you are beginning to believe they are true."

The knocking came again. More desperate this time, but weaker.

Bianca threw open the door. Whether it was a friend or a stranger, she would not leave someone standing on their front step in a thunderstorm. The wind ripped the door from her fingers and slammed it back against the wall. She stared at an ebony beast towering over her, its wings raised to swoop down on her. She backed away one step, then another.

"Who are you?" she cried.

The beast lurched toward her, raising huge paws. She froze, unable even to breathe. What sort of creature was it?

Bianca released a shuddering breath when the creature did not chase her. A wild beast would not knock on their door. She was letting Rosie's anxiety infect her with silly thoughts. She blinked and realized what she had taken for a pelt and wings was nothing but a rain-soaked cloak.

A man she did not know raised his right arm weakly. He stared at the floor, but flung his fist forward as if he thought the door still remained closed. Had his eyes been so blinded by the lightning that he could not see?

"Do you need help?" she asked over the wind's screech.

The man pushed back the cloak's hood. Ebony hair glinted in the light from the fire, but his face was covered with dirt and mud. Rocked by the force of the wind, he opened his mouth. No sound came out.

"Do you want to come in?" she asked.

Again she got no answer. Why did he remain mute? Mayhap he could not hear or speak. But why did he hesitate to come inside? She saw him wobble and guessed that after fighting the storm, he could go no farther.

"Sir, please come in!" She grasped his right sleeve. "Come in, for *I* am getting drenched!"

He lurched toward her a single step. His foot caught on the low threshold. He careened forward and struck her heavily. She rocked back, hitting the table. Anguish rushed down her leg as his left arm fell over her shoulder, as lifeless as a fish washed up on the shore and just as unsteady.

"Sir! Please! I cannot—" With a moan, she collapsed beneath him. She hit the floor hard.

Bright flashes of light burst in front of her eyes as his head struck her cheek. Her breath was knocked out of her as her ears rang from the jolt against the stone floor of the foyer. The man's legs pinned hers to the floor, and his head lolled on her arm.

He must have lost his senses because he did not move. She fought to escape from beneath the man, but she was not able to shove him aside. She tried to slide out from beneath him, then wrenched herself to one side. She winced when his left shoulder hit the floor as roughly as hers had. He moaned, and she cradled his head in her lap as she fought to fill her lungs with fresh air.

"Bianca! Get away! I shall—"

"No!" she cried as she looked up to see Rosie holding a lamp over her head. She was shocked. Her sister was seldom so daring; then she realized that Rosie would set aside her shyness to protect those she loved. Putting her hand on her own throbbing temple, she added in a lower voice, "He has swooned."

"Swooned?" Rosie edged closer, lowering the lamp. "What is wrong with him?"

"I am unsure." She blinked and tried to focus her eyes. When a hand settled on her shoulder, she looked up again to see her aunt regarding her with a worried expression.

Aunt Millicent asked, "How do you fare, Bianca?"

"I am fine." That was a lie, but she was surely in a better state than this stranger, who had not moved since falling over her. "Rosie, run upstairs and get a blanket for him. He must be soaked right to the skin."

While Rosie hurried up the stairs at the rear of the foyer, Bianca drew the cloak off the man. It reeked of mud, and she was not sure what else.

"Did he have a horse?" asked Aunt Millicent.

"I could not see."

"I will check. It should not be left out in the wind and rain."

As her aunt threw her crocheted shawl over her shoulders and opened the door to look out into the storm, Bianca stared at the man on the floor. She could not guess if he was young or old, for his black hair hid his features that were now facing away from her. She reached to turn him onto his back, but pulled back her hands as she saw the unmistakable stain of blood on his left sleeve. The dried blood had run from nearly his shoulder all the way down to the hem of his sleeve.

"Aunt Millicent . . ." She looked up to see her aunt had left. Aunt Millicent loved animals, and she would not allow this man's horse to remain out in the storm.

Bianca stared at the man and the caked blood on his sleeve. Although horrified, she did not hesitate. If he had been shot recently, the blood would not be so caked into the wool of his coat that the rain could not dislodge it. He must have been shot at least a day ago.

What had happened, and why had someone shot him? If he were a criminal—no, it did not matter what he was. He had been shot.

Worrying about where and why would gain her nothing now. She must help him regain his senses. Grasping his shoulders again, she pulled him toward her, so she could heave him onto his back. Every muscle strained as she tugged on him, but she did not relent.

Bianca gasped when the man's right arm encircled her shoulders as he rolled toward her. He pulled her down on top of him in a far-too intimate embrace.

"Sir, release me!" she cried. Suddenly she was aware of how alone she was with this stranger. Aunt Millicent had gone outside, Rosie was upstairs, and with the thunder rumbling overhead, even if she screamed neither of them would be able to hear her.

As the man's hand swept along her back in a bold caress that pressed her even more tightly to his hard body, his lips tilted in a smile. "Hush, my darling. Come closer. Let me taste the wine upon your lips. It shall be sweeter than that from any vineyard."

She tried to wiggle away, but his arm locked around her with a strength she had not expected. "Sir, we must get you off the floor, and—"

"The floor is fine, my darling. I shall let your softness comfort me, and my shoulder shall be your pillow when we lie together tonight." A lighthearted laugh drifted from him.

Bianca fought the heat rising through her at his inappropriate words. She was no light-skirt. "Sir—"

"You must call me Lucian, and I shall call you my darling."

"Lucian, please let me go!"

He did not heed her. His fingers tilted her mouth toward his, and his eyes opened. Their blue depths were clouded and unfocused. She gasped when she realized that his fingers were ablaze against her arms. Not with the heat of passion, but with fever. She stretched to brush her hand against his forehead. He moaned at her slight touch, releasing her. She edged back as fear strangled her.

Fever!

If this stranger had brought another fever to prey on who was left in her family, she could lose her sister and aunt as well. She wanted to shout for him to get up and leave right now before his fever had a chance to attack Rosie and Aunt Millicent, too.

The man muttered something, and his eyes rolled up before closing. His hands dropped to the floor with a thump.

Rosie rushed down the stairs.

"Stay back!" Bianca cried. "He is ill."

"Of course he is ill." She knelt, placing a brightly colored quilt on him. "Do you know this man, Bianca?"

"How would I know him? I have never seen him before."

"But I heard him call you 'darling.'"

"He is fevered. Other than his name, I doubt he knew what he was saying. Mayhap Lucian is not even his given name." Bianca brushed the man's wet and tangled hair away from his closed eyes. His face, which was as lifeless as the stones beneath him, was well made, with a strong nose and chin. Indeed, under other circumstances she would have labeled him handsome. However, just now all she wanted was for him to leave.

Aunt Millicent scurried back into the house, closing the door behind her. She shook water from her shawl before hanging it on a peg by the door again. "His horse is secured in the barn. It was standing right on the road, the reins on the ground. I fear this poor man has taken quite a tumble." She hesitated, then asked, "Is he floored?"

"What?" asked Rosie.

Aunt Millicent's smile came and went swiftly. "It means 'very intoxicated.' It is Town cant."

"He is not drunk; he is fevered. Both of you should stay away." Bianca pulled the quilt up beneath his chin. His clothes were well made, but filthy. The cuffs of his ebony coat were soaked, and his tan breeches had been ripped at one knee, most likely when he toppled from his horse. He must have been traveling a good distance, for the toes of his boots were scuffed.

"Why won't he wake?" Rosie asked. "Is he injured as well as ill? A wound could cause such a fever."

"Yes, he is injured." Bianca pointed to his left sleeve. She relaxed. Why hadn't she thought of how fever could come from such an injury? What had she heard it called? Leaden fever. "You can see where he has bled there. It would appear that he was shot."

"Shot?" Rosie's voice came out in an appalled squeak. "If he was set upon by a conveyancer—"

"Enough, Rosie," Aunt Millicent chided. "We need to be commonsensical, not let fancy take our thoughts where they do not belong. Bianca cannot even be certain he was shot until the wound is examined. We must tend to this man until he can regain his senses. Then you will have all the answers to your questions. Do you wish me to check him, Bianca?"

"No, I can do it." She flashed her aunt an uneasy smile. "I have no fear he will seize me again."

"Seize you?" Aunt Millicent wore the expression that showed she was not pleased.

"'Twas nothing. He is quite bereft of his senses."

But she was not bereft of hers, Bianca realized quickly. As she pulled back his coat and ran her hands along his ribs, she could not fail to notice firm muscles beneath his blue-striped waistcoat. The scents of mud and sweat flowed over her. He murmured something. Glad she could not understand what he said, for it was sure only to add to her disquiet, she checked his right arm, then turned to his left.

His arm seemed to be weighted with cannon balls as she lifted it enough so she could try to pull off his sleeve. It was lacquered to him with the dried blood, and he groaned when she tried to lower the sleeve. She would have to cut it off him, but that could wait until they got him off the chilly floor.

Aunt Millicent bent to check his legs, but Bianca said, "He walked in here, so his legs must be uninjured."

"He fell."

"He tripped."

She touched Bianca's face. When Bianca winced, she added, "You shall be wearing a bruise here."

"I shall be fine."

Bending over the man, Bianca noticed, for the first time, how his face was etched with pain. "His skin is very hot. He may be suffering from more than the wound that sent that blood spiraling down his arm." She shuddered as the memories of her parents' deaths rushed at her. Taking a deep breath, she came to her feet. "Aunt Millicent, you and Rosie must stay away, so you do not sicken."

"And what of you?" cried Rosie. She grasped Aunt Millicent's arm. "What if Bianca becomes ill?"

"We all have been near the man," Aunt Millicent said. "We all could sicken, so we must take turns watching over him and each other. I suspect his fever is from his injury." Her eyes narrowed. "It has been a very long time since I saw such a wound, but this man's arm looks as if it has been shot."

"That is what I feared," Bianca said.

The man stirred.

"Sir?" asked Bianca. "Lucian, can you speak?"

Only mumbles came from his parched lips. She rose and got her glass of lemonade. Holding it to his lips, she poured some into his mouth. He choked, then swallowed. He whispered something, then lost once more what little consciousness he had regained.

"Let us get him upstairs," Aunt Millicent said, taking a deep breath.

"Us? Carry him upstairs?" Rosie shook her head. "What if he comes to his senses and thrashes? We could drop him."

"You fret too much," Bianca said as she had before. "We need to get him upstairs and tend to him. Once he is awake, he will be able to get about on his own until he can return to where he belongs."

"If he wakes." Aunt Millicent bent to put her hands under his left shoulder. "Get his legs, girls."

Bianca picked up his right leg and asked, "What do you mean if he awakes?"

"He is grievously ill. I am not sure what turn this fever will take next."

She nodded. If the man died, they might have no

way of contacting **anyone** who knew him. He would die alone, far from his family and his friends . . . just as Kevin had.

Chapter Three

Was this hell? Was this unending throb of agony to be his punishment for the rest of eternity? Lucian wanted to believe it was not, but nothing formed in his head, save for the pain. He must escape it and discover what he had done to deserve this condemnation. After all, he had walked away from the duel with Andover, leaving the whelp of a cur alive.

"How does he fare?"

A woman's voice, barely louder than a whisper, rattled through his head and intruded into his dreams. Not dreams, but fiendish fragments of memory. His mind was mired in something as sticky as molasses, but finally he had understood something.

Words. Scents. Sensations. It was returning, pulling him back from the precipice of nothingness before he fell down, down, always down into the torment.

He relaxed and did not fight the pain. Letting it wash over him like an angry sea, yet hardly touching him as he floated on its currents, he fastened his thoughts on to the aroma of wood smoke and the tantalizing scent of meat cooking somewhere close by. Beneath him, something soft cradled him. He was warm. He was dry. The storm had vanished.

There had been times when he would have been

willing to wager his soul to be warm and dry, but since then he had returned to England. He should be grateful he had eluded Napoleon's death merchants and escaped from the storm. The respite from being battered by wind and rain should be enough, but it was not. He wanted to escape this pain.

Open your eyes.

The command came from within his head, startling him, for even the soft voice of his own thoughts had been silenced by the pain until now. He tried to obey, for then he might discover where he was and how he had gotten here.

His eyelids refused to move. Had they been sewn to his face?

"He is sleeping."

He was astonished. He recognized that soft, utterly feminine voice. Its husky warmth was as luscious and melodic as the first spring breeze. Where had he heard it before? In London? Mayhap so, but when? Certainly not since he had returned from the Continent, because he had not had the opportunity—or had not taken the opportunity—to enjoy the company of the fairer sex. Avoiding women as well as his own friends saved him from the questions he could not answer. For a nation that seemed otherwise eager to put the long war behind it, too many were interested in what he had done and what he had seen on the far side of the Channel. Explaining would be useless, because those who had remained safely in England could not begin to comprehend what he had experienced. It was better, he had decided within days of his arrival back in England, to avoid any situation where he might be asked about his service to the King.

A fire seared through Lucian's left arm when he

tried to move. A groan started in the center of his gut and erupted through his pounding skull. He had never hurt like this! What was wrong with him? Andover had not killed him . . . or had he? Was this some sort of hell he had been sent to?

Cool fingers brushed his forehead. The touch was a comfort and a torment, for even that light caress hurt. Yet something about those fingers was familiar. He had enjoyed their delightfully delicate caress before. A woman's touch. But who was she? He had no face to go with those gentle fingers.

He had to open his eyes.

"Lucian?"

Lucian? She was speaking to him. She knew his name. Mayhap she knew what had happened to him.

"Lucian, can you hear me?"

He must open his eyes. He *had* to see this woman and find out if her face matched the loveliness of her voice.

Sunshine burned his eyes as he forced them open, and he blinked, discovering that he was looking out a window draped with simple, unbleached muslin curtains. He started to look in the other direction, then halted as renewed pain lashed him. He stared at the simple walls beneath a low, slanting roof. But the walls that were painted a pale blue and the rafters rising at an angle with the ceiling were not what he wanted to see. Gritting his teeth, he slowly turned his head. The sound of the crisply starched pillowcase beneath his head sent more misery flooding over him.

He saw only gray. An apron, he realized, and he raised his gaze higher. Egad, why did his head have to ache at the mere thought of moving? A thin line of blue, as muted as the color on the wall, topped the gray. A light blue dress. It must be. He fought to focus his eyes and was rewarded with the sight of feminine curves above a modest bodice covered by the apron. He tried to fasten his gaze on the woman's face, but it was just a creamy cloud edged by red-gold.

"He is awake, Aunt Millicent." He recognized the voice. It was the one that had drawn him out of his agony. Now it was hushed, as if she comprehended how much he was suffering. Who was this woman?

"What of the fever?" asked the voice he had heard first. Another woman who must be talking to the woman beside his bed. He had no strength to look beyond this woman to the other. It did not matter. He wanted to see *this* woman.

"The fever is almost gone," she said, "so I believe he will survive."

Survive? Survive what? What in the name of Mad King George was wrong with him? He tried to ask, but his constricted throat cramped on the words.

The woman moved away, and a door opened and closed. He cursed silently. Her heart must be made of stone for her to leave him when he was at his weakest.

An arm slipped beneath his shoulders. He flinched at the gentle touch. An aroma, sweeter than the wood smoke and more tempting than the food cooking, filled every breath he drew. His cheek brushed silken strands of that amazing hair that was not auburn or tawny, but both. The woman! She had not left. It must have been the first woman—the one who asked how he fared—who had taken her leave.

"Drink," she whispered. "It will help."

He tried to look up at her, but she held a tin cup to

his lips, blocking his view. He drank. The thin broth soothed his ravaged throat.

"Who?" he asked, his head aching even though he spoke as softly as she had. "Who are you?"

"Bianca. Bianca Dunsworthy."

His next question caught in his throat, along with his breath, as she helped him lean back into the pillow, and finally he could see her face. She was an angel. He should have guessed that before, because he could not imagine any earthly woman with such hair. No, he told himself when her breath brushed his cheek, she was a living woman. Her hair drifted away from the ribbon trying to hold it back to wisp about her lightly pink cheeks. Her lips were tilted in a smile as he stared up into her earth brown eyes. Most definitely she was no angel, he could tell by the strong emotions in those eyes.

"You must rest, Lucian," she said in a voice meant to soothe him, but it had the opposite effect because he wanted to find out more about Bianca Dunsworthy. "You have been very ill."

"Ill?" He knew he sounded as witless as the king's fool.

"Quite ill, but your wound is healing, and you shall be better soon."

His fingers quivered like an old man's as he caught her hand before she could step away from the bed. Her eyes widened when he curled her fingers over his and, using his flagging reserves of strength, drew them to his mouth. The taste of her skin was more luscious and far more invigorating than the thin broth she had fed him.

Her brows arched as she drew her hand out of his with absolutely no effort. He must be far weaker than he had guessed, because he would have enjoyed holding those slender fingers longer.

"I see that you are better already." A hint of tartness whetted her voice.

He smiled, but did not reply that the very sight of such a beguiling woman was medicine enough to free a man from his deathbed. "Bianca?" he whispered, straining to say that much.

"You know my name. May I know yours?"

"Lucian Wandersee, fourth Earl of Wandersee."

"Earl?" Again her eyes grew wide.

He frowned, then wished he had not. Each motion sent more pain hurling across his forehead. "Why are you surprised? You must know who I am."

"Not until this moment, for you said nothing to identify yourself other than your name was Lucian."

He cursed the pain, refusing to let it stop him from obtaining what information he could. "Has Moss been ill as well, so he could not tell you my name?"

"Who is Moss?"

"My coachee." Every thought was more difficult to form than the one before it.

"Coachee? What is that?"

"My driver," he said with some heat when she regarded him with puzzlement.

She shook her head, and her face blurred when his eyes could not follow. "You did not arrive here in a carriage. You had a horse with you."

He was about to reply, but his thoughts slowed even further. Exasperation taunted him as his eyes closed. She must have added some medicinal herbs to the soup. He would not let her dupe him . . . not again.

* * *

"An earl?" Rosie stared at Bianca in astonishment. "Oh, my!"

"He said his name is Lord Wandersee." Bianca continued to peel the apples for the pie she was making for supper. "The fourth earl of that title, I believe he said."

"I have never met an earl before."

"Nor have I."

Rosie leaned her hands onto the flour-covered table. A dreamy expression came into her eyes. "Mayhap fairy tales do come true. You were telling a story about an earl, and one appeared at our door."

"Not by his choice." She laughed.

"You should not be amused at the poor man's situation."

"It was something he must have brought upon himself. Earls do not get shot in the arm for no reason."

"But if he was attacked by a highwayman, you would have more sympathy for him, wouldn't you?"

"Of course, but you know that we would have heard from Constable Powers if there was a knight of the pad preying on travelers along the shore road." Bianca chuckled again. "You know that the constable would have been anxious to keep *you* safe."

"Please, Bianca, no more jesting about Davis." A rush of color climbed Rosie's face.

Relenting, Bianca continued peeling the apples. The gawky, young constable who had taken over his duties in just the past year, seemed torn between concentrating on his work and courting Rosie. At every market day in the small village of Dunstanbury, Constable Powers found an excuse to speak with Rosie, who always seemed overmastered by his attentions and was almost mute. Bianca suspected the constable was unsure about whether Rosie welcomed his attentions or not, and she guessed that he had been about to ask Bianca that very question on more than one occasion. Each time, he had harrumphed, said something of no consequence, and hurriedly took his leave. Two such bashful people were an unlikely match.

She looked at her sister and sighed. Rosie was what the vicar called "husband-high." Constable Powers was not the only one who had taken note that the late baron's younger daughter had become a beauty. Mayhap it was time to speak with Aunt Millicent about looking for an appropriate match for Rosie—someone other than Constable Powers. She and the constable had known each other all their lives, for he had been born in Dunstanbury, and Rosie harbored a fantasy of a dashing hero sweeping her off her feet. Most importantly, Rosie's match should be someone who would understand she was not a wallflower, just quiet and unwilling to air her opinions for fear of hurting someone else.

Quite the opposite of Bianca. She smiled to herself as she scooped up the peelings and put them in a bucket next to the door where Mr. Chipman could collect them for his pigs. She never seemed uneasy about speaking her mind, as Rosie did. An exchange of contrasting ideas might develop into a brangle, but that did not intimidate her.

But she *was* intimidated by the thought of an earl lying upstairs asleep. Although she had been honest with Rosie—as she always was—she wondered if Lucian had been set upon by a highwayman. He had no purse with him, and Aunt Millicent had found no pack on his horse. If the earl had been traveling a great distance, he should have had some supplies and coin upon him. He could not be calling at Dunsworthy Hall, because her cousin was away. Also, word of such a visit would have spread through the village and along the shore with the speed of the lightning.

Had he been robbed and shot? Mayhap there was another explanation, but she could not guess what it was. She had little knowledge of the Polite World beyond what her mother had told her. Aunt Millicent seldom spoke of her Season, which had been curtailed by coming to take care of the orphaned baron and his sisters.

If Lucian was as outrageous with others as he had been with her . . . She gazed down at the hand he had kissed. The heat from his lips had not come from any fever, but the cursory caress had seared her skin. However a man should not be shot for daring to kiss a woman's hand with fervor. She did not want to imagine what could have persuaded someone to shoot him.

She shuddered at the thought. She needed to concentrate on her work, not on speculation. In quick order, she sliced the apples, and the pie was placed in the oven on one side of the kitchen hearth.

As Rosie cleaned the table so they might begin chopping vegetables for tonight's soup, she said, "I wonder if he is being honest."

"Why should he tell me lies?" Bianca asked, startled. It was unlike Rosie to be distrusting, for she customarily was too credulous.

"I am not suggesting he is telling you lies, but he may not be telling you the truth either."

"You are making no sense."

"That is exactly what I mean!"

"What?"

"Making no sense." Rosie stacked a handful of carrots and reached for some onions she had pulled in the garden. "He has had a debilitating fever, and he hit his head very hard when he bumped into you, as that bruise on your cheek shows. He might not have known what he was saying."

"I cannot argue with that, but I would have guessed that you, of all of us, Rosie, would believe that a fancy peer could land on our doorstep in the midst of a storm just like some hero in a fairy tale."

"I know the difference between fairy tales and the truth." A wistfulness filled her voice.

"What is wrong, Rosie?"

She shrugged, her lips trembling as tears filled her eyes. "I should have known better than to think that Mr. Pierce might have a *tendre* for me."

"Mr. Pierce? The blacksmith?" Bianca had never guessed that Rosie had any affection for the lumbering man who always stank, in Bianca's opinion, from the smoke in his smithy. "He was married last month to the youngest Adams girl."

"I know." She began to peel the onions, releasing their pungent scent into the kitchen. "He seems very happy."

"Why didn't you say anything about your affection for him before now?"

Again she shrugged. "There was nothing to say other than I thought he might have a *tendre* for me."

"Do you have one for him still?"

Rosie wiped tears from her cheeks, but Bianca guessed the tears were caused more by the onions than her distress, because Rosie said, "I am not sure."

"Not sure?"

"How does one know when one is in love?"

Aunt Millicent laughed as she came in the back door from the kitchen garden. "Go ahead, Bianca, and answer that question."

"I have no answer," Bianca said, smiling.

"Probably because that is one of the great questions of all times and a question that has no single answer."

Taking the bucket of fresh vegetables from her aunt, Bianca asked, "What do you mean?"

"Falling in love has different symptoms for each person." She drew off the gloves she used for gardening. Once they had been lovely kid gloves, but now they were cracked and gray from use. She put them and her work bonnet on the shelf by the door and ladled a cup of water from the pail that Bianca had drawn from the well that afternoon. "I have seen a man and a woman argue constantly, but they are deeply devoted to each other."

"Like The Raven and The Dog innkeeper and his wife." Rosie giggled. "They never speak to each other in less than a shout."

Aunt Millicent sat on the high stool by the dry sink and took a slow, appreciative drink. "Then there is the butcher and his wife, who seldom speak to each other in their shop, but have twelve children with another one on the way. It is obvious when you see them away from the shop with the children that they are a very happy family."

"Were you ever in love, Aunt Millicent?" Rosie asked, her eyes now aglitter with delight at talking about this topic. She ignored the tears flooding her cheeks.

Taking pity on her sister, Bianca took the knife and began chopping the onions. She was surprised when her aunt did not come back with a quick answer, because Aunt Millicent seldom was without a response to anything. Her eyes widened. Her aunt was wearing an expression as dreamy as Rosie's when Bianca told a tale of an assembly in a fine manor house. Was her aunt remembering something wondrous from her past?

"Aunt Millicent?" she asked quietly.

Her aunt flinched, then shook herself as if coming awake. *Or from the depths of some precious memory,* Bianca added silently.

"Pardon me. Just thinking." She took a hasty sip, then stared down at her empty cup.

With a laugh, Rosie refilled it and handed it back to her aunt. "Will you share those thoughts with us, Aunt Millicent? Mayhap they will help me get an answer to my impossible question."

"Why not? You are not children any longer." Setting the heels of her low boots on one rung of the stool, she rested the cup on her knees. "I was in love once. I was quite mad for the man."

"Who?" asked Rosie as she sat on the edge of the hearth.

"His name is not important."

"Aunt Millicent!"

Her aunt smiled at Rosie's frustration. "Very well, let me see. I believe his name was Quinn."

"How could you forget his name?" Rosie stared at her in disbelief.

"It has been almost fifteen years since I last spoke with him."

Wiping her teary eyes and runny nose, Bianca asked, "Why didn't you marry him?"

"He was only a few years older than I am, and, at the time, his mother deemed him too young to wed."

She stared down into the cup. "I have not seen him since the last time I visited London."

"Giving up so easily does not sound like you," Bianca said. "You have taught us that we should not let anything keep us from doing what is right."

Aunt Millicent arched a golden brow. "I did not give up easily. His mother was a termagant, and her temper was more fierce than even the Dunsworthy one. We had words—very loud words, I must own—and said hateful things. I thought it best not to return."

"Has he married since?"

"I don't know. I have not heard one way or the other." Her lighthearted laugh returned. "*On dits* from London very seldom finds their way to Dunsworthy Dower Cottage. It hardly matters, for that is in the past."

Bianca exchanged a glance with her sister. Rosie had a twinkle in her eyes that disclosed her thoughts were very much like Bianca's. There must be a way to find out if the gentleman named Quinn had wed. After all, it was not a common name. No matter how much Aunt Millicent professed that she was uninterested, Bianca could not forget her aunt's sad, distant expression when Rosie had asked if she had ever fallen in love.

"How many onions are you chopping?" asked Aunt Millicent as she wiped her own eyes. "That pile seems twice as high as usual."

Bianca put down her knife. "Lord Wandersee has regained his senses, although he is sleeping now, and I suspect, once he is fully alert, he will be very hungry."

"*Lord* Wandersee?" Aunt Millicent's face blanched. "Are you telling me that our guest is a lord?"

"An earl!" Rosie replied excitedly, acting as if she had never expressed any doubts about the veracity of their patient's claim.

"Oh, dear, I suppose we should alert Constable Powers. After seeing the wound in his arm, I had thought our guest might be a poacher shot while hunting where he should not, so I delayed sending for the constable."

Bianca put the onions into the cast-iron pot that would be hung on the iron arm over the fire. She understood her aunt's hesitation, for poachers could be transported from England for their crime. "I doubt poachers wear clothing as fine as his."

"It could have been stolen," Rosie averred.

"No, I don't think so. He speaks with a sense of command that one would not expect to hear a poacher use, and his voice is definitely quality."

Aunt Millicent stood. "I must go and speak with Constable Powers. If an earl is missing and nobody has come in search of him, there must be something terribly amiss."

"Something unsavory?" asked Rosie.

Patting her younger niece's shoulder, she laughed. "I doubt it, but I want to let the constable know Lord Wandersee is here in case someone comes seeking his help to find our guest." She took her bonnet off the shelf. "I shall not be long."

For a moment, Bianca thought that her sister would ask to walk with Aunt Millicent into the village and to the small house where the constable resided. Then Rosie glanced at the ceiling and sighed. Leaving Bianca alone here when there was a strange man in a bedroom above was out of the question.

After Aunt Millicent left, Bianca continued preparing the vegetables while Rosie stirred the broth and seasoned it. Soon it was bubbling over the fire, and the apple pie was browning nicely in the oven.

At the sound of knuckles rapping on the kitchen door, Bianca exchanged a startled look with her sister. No one knocked at the back door. Going to it, she opened the door.

A dark-haired man she did not recognize tipped his hat to her. He was dressed in a simple dark green livery that had seen rough use and appeared to have been slept in. He was not young, probably close to the age her father would have been now.

"Good afternoon," she said when he did not speak.

Tipping his cap, he replied, "Good afternoon, miss. I was wondering if you might help me."

"If I can. What do you need?"

"I am looking for a gentleman."

She smiled. "You must be Moss."

The man's long face eased from its tense lines. "That you know my name, miss, tells me that the gentleman I seek has been here. Is he still within?"

As Rosie stared at the man, her eyes huge and her mouth clamped closed with her shyness, Bianca motioned for Moss to come in. The coachman knocked dust from his boots before he entered. After he had glanced around the cheerful kitchen, he looked at her anxiously.

"Yes, he is here." Bianca faltered, then said, "He has been a bit befuddled with his fever. Is his name truly Lucian Wandersee?"

"Yes, and I am his coachman." Moss's grin was so broad that she feared his face would not be able to hold it. "I have been looking everywhere around the village for Lord Wandersee."

Bianca heard her sister's sharp intake of breath at Moss's confirmation of what Lucian had told her. Mayhap Rosie would not have been so averse to believing that Lucian possessed a title if she had spoken with him herself when he woke.

"He arrived here in the midst of the thunderstorm two nights ago," she replied. "He has been very ill."

"A fever?"

"Yes."

"How does he fare?" he asked with such reluctance that she knew he dreaded her answer.

"The fever is gone, and we have redressed the wound on his arm."

Moss released his breath in a whoosh that sounded as if one of his horses had appeared in the kitchen. "That is the best tidings I have heard in many an hour, Miss . . ."

"Dunsworthy." She introduced herself and her sister. "How was it that Lord Wandersee was wandering—" She smiled when Moss grinned. "How was it that he was out in such a storm when he was half mad with fever?"

"He went to his room at the inn in the village as soon as we had stopped for the night." He kneaded his chin, which was prickly with whiskers. "The Raven and The Dog, isn't it called?"

"Yes."

"I thought he might be hungry, even though he was feeling poorly, so I had a tray sent up to him. The serving lass came back with the word that he was not in his room. A search of the inn revealed that Lord Wandersee was nowhere to be found." Moss sighed, and she could imagine his despair at having his master vanish. "A lad in the stables said a man had asked for a horse and had ridden away."

"But to where was he bound?"

Moss shook his head. "I have no idea. The lad said that his lordship repeated over and over that he had to get there before it was too late."

"Too late? Do you know what he meant by that?"

"It makes no sense to me, Miss Dunsworthy, because he is on his way to attend a gathering at a friend's house farther west along the shore. It would not matter if he were even a day or two late. Such a party will go on for as long as there are guests. To be honest, we would have arrived there nearly a fortnight early." He began to say something else, then coughed.

Bianca jabbed Rosie with her elbow and pointed at the water bucket. Her sister filled a cup. Gingerly she handed it to the coachman. He thanked her, then took a deep drink.

"Just the thing," he said. " 'Tis been a long, hot, very dry day driving every road in this shire looking for my lord. Now that I have found him, I can take him back to The Raven and The Dog and relieve you of tending to him further. If you will take me to him, Miss Dunsworthy . . ."

"He is not yet ready to travel. He is sleeping now." Bianca perched on the stool where her aunt had been sitting, then gasped. "Rosie, Aunt Millicent needs to be halted before she alerts the constable."

Moss put down his cup. "I will be glad to drive you wherever you need to go, miss."

"I can reach her faster across the fields," Rosie said and, grabbing her own bonnet, ran out the back door.

Stirring the soup and checking on the pie, Bianca

asked in the most casual tone she could, "Moss, would you answer one question for me?"

"Of course, Miss Dunsworthy."

"How did Lord Wandersee come to be shot in the arm?"

He glanced at the bench by the door, and she motioned for him to sit. As he did, he said, "Well, Miss Dunsworthy, it is quite a tale, it is. I vow to you that 'tis the truth, although I swear I would not have believed it myself if I had not been a witness." He explained what had happened outside his lord's club in London.

"A duel?"

"Yes."

"In the middle of a London street?"

Moss nodded. "I would understand if you accused me of telling you out-and-outers, Miss Dunsworthy, but what I have told you is the truth. It is fortunate that my lord was able to maintain his composure when he was provoked, or the situation might have been even worse."

"It is still not over," she said. "He is quite ill even now, even though he is no longer suffering from his feverish delusions."

The coachee's face fell, and she wished she had spoken with more care. There must be some words to comfort him, but she was unsure what they might be. Moss must wait, as the rest of them did, to see if Lucian could overcome the wounds and the madness of his ride out into the storm. She hoped when Lucian regained his full senses, he would explain why he had risked his life for a reason none of them could understand.

Chapter Four

Lucian opened his eyes and smiled. The worst of the pain in his head was gone. His left arm throbbed with a deep, dull agony, but it was something he could tolerate. Shadows laced through the rafters sloping over his bed. Looking across the narrow room, he was pleased to discover how easy it was to move his head. He wanted to shout and sing and celebrate, but he simply smiled. He honestly doubted he had the energy to do much more.

"You must be feeling better."

His smile broadened. He recognized the woman by her voice and hair, which was the color of the sky just before the sunset gave way to the night's blue, a deep luscious gold laced with red. She was the woman who had tended to him. Her name was . . . Her name refused to come forth from his unsteady brain.

Shifting his head so he could look up at her, he noticed for the first time a handful of freckles sprinkled across her nose. They added a pertness to her face and lessened the strain of sleeplessness that had left gray arcs beneath her eyes. Was that a bruise on one cheek? If she had a heavy-handed husband, Lucian vowed to discuss gentlemanly behavior with the lout. It was the very least he could do for this woman who had nursed him back from the doorway of death. He would tend to that matter . . . as soon as he could get out of this bed.

"Yes." His voice cracked on the single word. Vexed, he struggled to add, "I am doing better."

"Thirsty?" she asked.

"Yes!"

"Hungry?"

"Yes!"

"Good." She chuckled. "Please do not think I am glad that you are hungry and thirsty. They are simply signs—"

"That I am better."

She recoiled, and he guessed he sounded too petulant. Dash it! Here he was imprisoned in this bed in this unknown house, and she seemed to expect him to be the pattern-card of etiquette.

Instantly, he negated that thought. Those gray circles under her eyes revealed that she had been taking care of him at the expense of her own sleep. Her few words and his blasted debility divulged, as well, that he must have been in great danger of dying from whatever had sapped him. He should act grateful, for he was.

"Forgive me . . ." Lucian searched his mind for her name. When she opened her mouth, he held up his hand. Frowning when he saw how it shook as if with palsy, he said, "Forgive me, Miss Dunsworthy. I am deeply appreciative of the kindness you have shown me in what was clearly my hour of need."

"Your two days of need."

"Two days?" he choked. He had been lost in the nether world of that accursed fever for two full days?

"Do not think about that now. Think now only of

your good fortune that you are recovering," she said, patting his hand.

He uncurled his fingers to entangle them with hers. In the moment before she drew them away, they quivered as his had. *She* was not suffering from a fever, so that tremor must have been because of his touch. That thought pleased him and sent an invigorating pulse through him. With clear eyes, he admired the slender curves so close to where he was lying. Not even her simple gown could diminish the grace of each motion.

"Where are we?" he asked, determined to keep her here by his bed as long as he was able. The sight of her was, without question, the best medicine a man could have.

"Dunsworthy Dower Cottage," she replied, her voice still hushed.

"Where is that?"

"Our cottage is set back from the shore road about two days' journey east of Plymouth. Most people pass by here and the village farther inland without taking any notice of us." She smiled. "However, you found us during the storm, and your coachman arrived while you were asleep."

"Moss is here?" That was the best news he had heard since he had regained his senses.

"He brought your carriage from The Raven and The Dog. The inn on the shore road," she added, and he guessed she had seen his confusion. "Do you think you can sit? You must be able to sit up and show that you have recovered your wits if you want to get out of that bed."

"Or get you in it." The words were spoken before he could halt them.

Her lips tightened into a scowl, and she folded her arms in front of her bodice. "You can be assured, my lord, that I have no interest in tending to you *that* way. If your thoughts are wandering in that direction, then I suspect you are hale enough not to need my tending in any way."

When she turned to leave, he caught her hand. "Miss Dunsworthy, forgive me. My mouth seems to be working at a pace different from my mind. I apologize for offending you, although my intentions would have been—"

"You have made your intentions quite clear."

"My intentions," he said as if she had not spoken, "were to compliment you." He resisted the temptation to stroke her fingers. Dash it, she was lovely. Far too lovely to intrude on his life when he wanted to keep it free of complications.

"You have a peculiar way of complimenting a woman," she said, her voice still prim.

"You can be assured that my thoughts will remain hidden within my battered skull from this point forward, Miss Dunsworthy." He smiled. "After all, if a man were to be condemned solely on his thoughts in the company of a charming woman, there would not be one of us alive."

"You are glib."

"Does that mean I am forgiven?"

"I would not go so far as to say that, but if you refrain from making such comments again, I will forget this one."

He had to own that he was startled she was so magnanimous, for his comment had been vulgar, especially to a country miss who would be unfamiliar with the flirting the Polite World took for granted.

"Most kind of you. Now will you help me sit?" He held up his right arm. His left one still hurt too much to move unless absolutely necessary.

Instead of giving him a quick retort, Miss Dunsworthy glanced toward the door past the hearth that filled the whole wall opposite the single window. He wondered if she might be seeking the other woman who had been with her when he had been awake before. Mayhap she was contemplating sending for Moss. That made sense, but Lucian did not want his coachman here when he could enjoy talking alone to this pretty young woman.

When her gaze flickered back toward him, he saw conflicting emotions flashing through her eloquent eyes. This woman never would be able to cloak her feelings, but was that because of innocence or insouciant worldliness? He was curious to discover which.

"Yes, I will help you," she said as she bent to slide her arm beneath him. "You must promise to keep your mind and mouth working in unison."

"I shall endeavor to do so."

Her soft cheek brushed his bewhiskered one, and she pulled back, alarm in her eyes. *Innocence*, he thought, intrigued.

"You have to help, too," she murmured.

He smiled as her words caressed his ear. Mayhap she was not so innocent, after all. "I shall endeavor to do so," he repeated.

Giving him an odd glance, she said only, "Good."

Again she put her arm around his shoulders. He pressed against the mattress to push himself up to sit. When her bewitchingly soft curves grazed his arm, he slipped his arm around her waist. She tensed, but did not release him. He forgot his pleasure with her touch as renewed agony swelled through his head.

Blast Andover! This was the first time Lucian had been so close to an enticing young woman in longer than he wished to recall, and the wound in his arm was demanding too much of his attention. If Andover had not shot him . . . He was making no sense. If Andover had not shot him, he would have had no reason to be in Miss Dunsworthy's kind care.

He pushed all such absurd thoughts from his head as he concentrated on sitting. It was taking far more of his strength than he had expected. Panting with exertion when he was propped against the plain headboard, he said, "Thank you for your help. I am weaker than I guessed."

"You have been very sick. The wound in your arm festered, and it brought on a fever. You were quite out of your head when you arrived here."

He sought to recall anything about coming to this cottage, but his memory refused to disgorge anything much of what had happened after leaving London. He waited for the facts to rush out of his mind like an icy wind, clearing his head. He could recall Andover's challenge and the gun firing on St. James's Street. Beyond that, he was less sure of what he recalled. Blast Andover!

"You could have died," Miss Dunsworthy continued as she tucked the covers around him and back beneath the mattress. "According to Moss, you rode away from The Raven and The Dog in a feverish haze when you were supposed to be resting in your room."

"That was a foolish thing to do."

"I agree." A hint of a smile returned to her face. "Do you recall why you did so?"

"No."

She frowned. "Nothing?"

"Miss Dunsworthy, your expression tells me that you believe I am being less than honest with you. It is my misfortune that I am being completely honest. I do not recall arriving at this tavern you speak of, nor do I recall leaving it."

"Oh, I see." She drew back, and he wondered if his voice had been too honed again.

He had every right to be frustrated. Two days of his life had vanished, thanks to Andover's drunken duel. How many more must he waste in recovery from this hole in his arm? His vexation eased when he saw Miss Dunsworthy regarding him with sympathy.

"I must have been very ill," he said, uncertain how else to shatter the silence that seemed to be smothering them.

"Out of your mind with fever is closer to the truth, my lord."

While she plumped up a pillow and put it behind him, he smiled at her. She was not tall, but she still could walk upright in only half the room. His gaze slid along the apron that was pinned to her unadorned bodice.

"I will send your coachman up to speak with you, if you are ready to have callers," she said, her voice once again as starched as the linens beneath him.

"Yes—thank you." He added the last when she turned away.

Bianca filled a tin cup from a pitcher on a small table by the window and took it back to Lord Wandersee. She was proud of how she was controlling her emotions when her hand did not tremble. "You are welcome."

She took a step back from the bed, then heard him curse. Glancing over her shoulder, she saw that specks of water had splashed over his right sleeve. He was glowering at the cup as if it had betrayed him.

"It is my turn to ask you to forgive me," she said softly as she brought a cloth from the table. Dabbing it at his sleeve, she took the cup from him. "I should not have filled the cup so full when you are as weak as a newborn pup."

He looked up at her, and she was caught by the rage in his blue-gray eyes. Her heart lost a beat before she realized that his anger was turned inward. He was furious at himself and the foolish lord who had shot him. Now that he was awake, she could not ignore the aura of strength this earl possessed. And his touch . . .

She took the damp cloth and hung it by the hearth. Mayhap, with her face so flushed that it burned, she could blame its heat on the fire. Into another cup she spooned a single ladle of the vegetable soup from the pot being kept warm there. She carried it carefully to the bed.

He held out his hands. She was going to ask if he thought he could manage even this half-filled cup when he was so feeble, but one glance into those compelling eyes warned her not to come too close again. There was no threat in them that urged her away; it was the quickening of her own heartbeat. How could it be fluttering as wildly as a caged bird when her gaze met his? She avoided answering that question as she handed him the soup and a spoon.

He took a bite and said, "Very good. Is it your receipt?"

"It is Rosie's. She enjoys working with the kitchen much more than I ever have."

"Rosie?"

"My sister." She glanced toward the window, where ruddy light from the setting sun splattered onto the floor. "Primrose Dunsworthy."

Lord Wandersee shifted, sitting straighter. "Did I hear you talking to her when I first awoke?"

"You probably heard my aunt. Millicent Dunsworthy. She has been helping with your care."

"And your uncle?"

"Aunt Millicent is unwed." She hesitated when his eyes became slits. Had she said too much? Nonsense! He would see the facts for himself as soon as he was able to get out of bed.

"Three spinsters?" Lord Wandersee laughed, astonishing her, for the sound was stronger than she had guessed it might be. "If I had to take ill, I chose the right place."

"You were not so much ill as wounded."

"True."

"And you were fortunate to find shelter in that storm. Why were you wandering about on such a horrible night?"

He handed her back the now-empty cup. Wiping his hand against the ebony shadow along his upper lip, he touched his head. His brow rutted, and she guessed his pain had returned. She thought of telling him that rest and quiet would ease that pain, but suspected he would be unhappy with such a prescription.

"As I told you," he said, "my thoughts are a jumble of twisted strands of thread. I cannot tell the difference between a true memory and what may be only part of a nightmare."

"Moss explained to us that you told a stable lad at The Raven and The Dog that you were afraid you were going to be too late."

Bianca had heard the description of a face closing up before, but she doubted she had ever understood it until now. All expression vanished from Lord Wandersee's features, leaving them a lifeless mask. His gaze had turned inward, and she suspected he understood exactly why he had spoken those words.

What was he doing here so far from London? Moss had mentioned a journey to visit a friend, but the coachman had not said exactly where. Moss *had* mentioned that Lord Wandersee did not need to reach that friend's house for two weeks. Had the earl planned to stop somewhere along the way for some reason only he could know? Curiosity teased her, but she silenced it. Even though his manners had been less than polished since he had regained his senses, she would not be rude enough to quiz him about what he had meant when he declared himself too late. *She* had not been injured, so she could not blame her vulgar questions on an aching head.

She picked up his boots. When he asked where she was taking them, she said, "Your coachee offered to give them a good polish when I told him about their condition."

"Condition? My boots always have an excellent shine." He smiled, but his eyes still were filled with powerful emotions she could not decipher. "A habit I had refined for me while in the King's service."

"You were in the army?"

"Yes." He touched the bandage on his left arm.

"Did you serve on the Continent?"

"Yes. Ironic, isn't it? I escaped that without much

more than a scratch. It is when I am in London that I am shot by some deranged baron who thinks I wish to steal his adulterous mistress."

"Moss told me about that absurd duel. Were you out of your mind to agree to such a thing?" She set the boots on the blanket chest at the foot of the bed. "You were lucky you were not killed when you were facing a superior marksman."

He started to cross his arms, then winced. Cradling his left elbow, he retorted, "Mayhap Moss did not tell you that I was trying to protect a friend who was suffering from what I fear were heart palpitations."

"Really?" Bianca let her shoulders untense from their stiff, angry pose. "I am so sorry, my lord, that I assumed you were simply foolish."

"You had every right to assume that. I have been at far less than my best since I woke here."

She picked up the boots again. "Let me take these down to Moss. You must have traveled a long way in these."

"May I see them?" Taking one, he examined the scuffed toes. "How far is the inn . . . What did you call it?"

"The Raven and The Dog."

"Charming name." He handed the boot back to her. "How far is it from this cottage?"

"Not far."

Lucian searched his mind for an elusive memory. "If I walked along the shore, the sand and pebbles would have stolen the polish from my boots."

"But you were riding."

"I had a horse with me, but you cannot assume I was riding by the time I reached your cottage."

She regarded him without expression, then a hint

of a smile tilted her lips. "That is true, but then one must ask why you were walking through a storm when you had a horse?"

"That I cannot answer, Miss Dunsworthy." He hated lying to her, but he owed her a duty for saving his life. He would be beneath reproach to add to that debt by speaking of the very matters that had led him to avoid his closest friends in London. Now that the war was over, everyone in England just wanted to forget. He wished he could, too.

With a sigh, he watched her walk away from the bed. Admiring the gentle sway of her skirt drew him away from his doldrums. When she glanced out the window, he asked, "Are you looking for someone?"

"Rosie and Aunt Millicent took a pot of soup to our neighbor, Widow Morehouse. We try to visit her once a week to be certain she is well. They should be back soon."

"So you were left alone to tend to me?" He smiled as she glanced over her shoulder in astonishment. That fetching color painted her cheeks.

"Of course not. Your coachman is here to serve as a watch-dog to give countenance to the whole of this. Now that you are awake, you shall soon meet Aunt Millicent and Rosie." A knock sounded on the door, and she whirled to open it with a speed that suggested she was relieved not to be alone with him.

The pulse of irritation at that thought vanished when Lucian saw Moss standing in the doorway. His coachee was wringing his cap, as he did whenever he was distressed. Nodding to Miss Dunsworthy, Moss said, "Lord Wandersee, it is good to see you sitting up!"

"It is good to be back among the living," he answered.

Miss Dunsworthy handed Moss the boots, and the coachee smiled at her. Lucian would have fallen off his feet with amazement if he had been standing. Moss was a great coachman, but he was as stolid as a stone. Although Moss had been driving for Lucian for almost a decade, Lucian guessed he could count on both hands the number of times he had seen the coachee smile. Now Moss was smiling at Miss Dunsworthy as he had done so often. He watched how kindly Miss Dunsworthy thanked Moss, and he chuckled under his breath as he wondered how she had endeared herself so quickly to the morose Moss.

The answer was simple: just as she had charmed him, she had charmed his coachman. A country lass could better herself with a marriage to an upper servant in a grand house.

Moss and Miss Dunsworthy? Lucian did not like that thought for many reasons. Foremost was because of how he himself found her touch pleasing.

"Miss Dunsworthy and her family have taken good care of you, my lord." Moss's voice brought his attention back to his coachman.

Lucian frowned. Miss Dunsworthy was not in the room. Blast! His drifting thoughts had kept him from taking note of when she left.

"Is there something wrong?" asked Moss, who was unable to stand completely straight in the low-ceiling room.

Lucian knew his expression was about to betray his thoughts. "What is wrong today is far less than what was wrong yesterday."

Moss plucked at the top of one boot as if it were a harp. "I am glad to hear that, my lord."

"Spit it out, man." He was seldom vexed with his coachman, but when Moss hesitated to speak about something that was bothering him—as he was now—Lucian found him exasperating.

"I am sorry I did not see how poorly you were feeling."

"You are not my nursemaid, Moss." He looked down at his left arm. "I could have asked for help."

"But when you were so out of your mind with fever that you mistook Miss Dunsworthy for a cyprian—"

Lucian sat straighter, ignoring the blaze of pain at his sudden motion. "I did what?"

"Miss Millicent Dunsworthy spoke of the incident to show me how sick you had been, my lord."

"What did I say?"

Moss shuffled his feet, but Lucian saw a hint of a smile on his coachman's face. "Not only what you said, but what you did."

Lucian groaned when Moss had finished explaining how he had embraced Miss Dunsworthy and tried to kiss her. If Miss Dunsworthy had been willing to forgive him for treating her with such familiarity the night he arrived, he understood why she had been prepared to forgive him today. He must find a way to atone for his ill-mannered actions at the same time he kept his tongue between his teeth. Admiring Miss Dunsworthy and imagining that he held her was one thing; speaking of those fantasies was quite another.

"Thank you, Moss," he said as he cradled his aching arm against his chest. "I shall endeavor to recall that Miss Dunsworthy may not be familiar with the oft-foolish ways of the *ton*."

"That may not be exactly true."

"And what information do you have, Moss, that you want me to have so badly that you are lingering here when I know you would prefer to be somewhere where you could stand upright without crouching?" He smiled. "Or perchance are you waiting for Miss Dunsworthy to return? I have to own that she seems to have charmed you very quickly. Be wary of her, Moss. You do not have a fever's madness to use as an excuse if you want to kiss her."

"Kiss Miss Dunsworthy?" The coachman's face became gray. "My lord, I would not even let the thought of such an action into my head."

"Why not? She is a comely lass, and you smile like the king's fool when she is near."

Moss squared his shoulders and hit his head against the low ceiling. In his sternest voice, he said, "She is kind-hearted and welcomed me within this house when I came here in search of you. However, even if I harbored more than gratitude for her welcome, I would never construe that kindness to be anything else when there is such a difference between her class and my own."

"Her class?" Lucian's smile faded. "Moss, I never thought of you as a high stickler who would look down at others. It is not a pleasing aspect."

"You mistake my words, my lord. I am not looking down at Miss Dunsworthy because she is of a lower class. Quite the opposite, for she is a baron's daughter."

Lucian was speechless, a most uncommon circumstance. A baron's daughter? Why was a baron's daughter living in a simple cottage like this? Mayhap she had said something, and he had missed it in the midst of his fever. He searched his mind, but found no memory of Miss Dunsworthy speaking of her father. She had talked only about her aunt and her sister. This was most peculiar.

Most peculiar and a most challenging puzzle to discover why she had failed to mention the truth to him while Moss had been told. He enjoyed a challenge, and this would be a good one when he could not get out of bed.

Dunsworthy. He could not recall the name being spoken in London, and it was the rare family that did not come under discussion by the *ton* at some time or other. A baron who had such a lovely daughter and did not bring her to Town for the Season would be a curiosity much discussed by the Polite World.

He looked up when Moss excused himself just as Miss Dunsworthy came back into the room. Nothing about her suggested she was anything other than the country miss he had assumed her to be. Her clothing was clean, but simple. She had none of the simpering airs too many young misses thought they should acquire for the Season. Nor had she turned an appraising eye upon him to measure his worth as a husband. He almost laughed at that thought. His indecorous actions and comments must have convinced her that she would be wise to rid her life of him with all possible speed.

Miss Dunsworthy gave him a smile as she asked him how he felt. Before he could answer, she asked, "My lord, would you care for more soup before I leave you to your rest?"

"If you do not mind," he replied, although he doubted he could rest now when so many thoughts were scurrying through his head.

"I would not have asked if I had minded."

He laughed. "Are you usually so forthright, Miss Dunsworthy?"

She took the cup and refilled it halfway. "It is a fault I cannot seem to overcome."

"I hope it was not the cause of that bruise on your face." He decided he could be as blunt as she was. Moss had not mentioned Miss Dunsworthy's cheek, so Lucian must find the truth of that himself.

"What?"

"It appears 'twas a heavy hand that struck you. Tell me the cur's name, and I shall advise him on how a woman should be gently treated."

She laughed, surprising him. Not just that she was amused, but how delighted he was with the transformation her smile brought to her face. Although he had noted from the moment he opened his eyes that she was lovely, her laughter sparkled like foam flying up from a wave and lit her face as if the sun had decided to focus its glow upon her. She handed him the cup, almost spilling soup on him because her hand shook with her laughter.

" 'Twas not a heavy hand," she said, "but a hard head."

"What? Whose?"

"Yours, my lord. You tumbled forward when you entered the house, and your head struck my cheek. I thank you for your gallantry, but it is unnecessary, for the culprit was not himself at the time."

Her laughter faded when he grasped her fingers with his left hand. As he had guessed, she did not dare to tug away, fearing that not only would she cause him to shower himself with soup, but that her action might injure his wounded arm. Taking the cup from him, she stretched to place it on the table, when he did not release her fingers.

"I am sorry, Miss Dunsworthy, for anything boorish that I said and did that night," he said in barely more than a whisper. "I can assure you that if I had been myself, as you put it so generously, I would have cut off my left arm before I would have hurt you."

"I know that." Her voice was as hushed as his, each word slipping along him like a cat's purring caress.

"Lucian."

"What?"

"Call me Lucian, and grant me the privilege of calling you Bianca. You have tended to me, and it seems a bit absurd to address each other as strangers."

"But we *are* strangers."

Before he could answer, a soft knock came from the door. He looked past Bianca to see two other women in the doorway. Her sister and her aunt, he suspected, when the younger's eyes grew round, and the elder woman's frown was replacing her smile. Did anyone else live with them in this house?

"You must be Primrose and Millicent Dunsworthy," Lucian said as if it were quite commonplace to find Bianca holding his hand.

"Yes." Miss Millicent Dunsworthy's tone and her rigid motions as she took off her poke bonnet warned she was furious with Lucian for his bold actions. Her eyes grew as large as Miss Primrose's had when he took her hand and raised it to his lips, holding it only for the length of time propriety suggested. A smile quirked on her lips. "You have much London polish, Lord Wandersee."

"I am not sure if you judge that comment a compliment or an insult, Miss Dunsworthy." He would address Millicent Dunsworthy that way. Bianca's younger sister would be properly addressed as Miss Primrose. And Bianca . . . She had not granted him permission to use her given name, but he found it very pleasurable to think of her as Bianca.

"A bit of both," Miss Dunsworthy replied.

"I see that being outspoken is a family trait."

"I am not sure if you judge that comment a compliment or an insult." She laughed.

"A compliment, most assuredly." He smiled at Bianca. "I appreciate your excellent care that saved my life."

Miss Dunsworthy drew the youngest woman forward and nudged her with her elbow. Miss Primrose clasped her hands in front of her and looked at the floor.

"She is very shy," Bianca said in a whisper as she pretended to plump up his pillow again. "Please treat her gently."

Lucian frowned at the suggestion that he would be less than a gentleman with her sister. How could he fault her when he had been a rough diamond with Bianca? Not just once, but twice. Blast! He had gotten off to an appalling beginning with this family.

Knowing he must say something to break the silence, Lucian said, "Bianca tells me that the soup I have been enjoying is your receipt, Miss Primrose."

"I am pleased that you liked it." She glanced up when he used her sister's name, then quickly looked back at the floor.

"Liked it? I hope I can persuade you to share the receipt with my kitchen so I may relish it again."

"Of course." She continued to stare at the tips of her slippers.

He heard Bianca's soft sigh. For such an outspoken woman, having a shy sister must be incomprehensible.

"Was that thyme I tasted in it?" Lucian asked.

"Yes." Miss Primrose's eyes flicked up again, then back down.

"And there was some other spice? What was it?"

"Either ginger or sage," she said quietly, but this time when her eyes rose, they did not focus on the floor again. "I am pleased you liked it."

Lucian saw wonderment on Bianca's face at her sister's replies. She was pleased, he could tell, that Miss Primrose was talking to him. He had many questions about this family and the puzzle they presented, and he doubted he would get answers from shy Miss Primrose or her aunt, who was trying to be polite by not scolding him for being forward with her niece. That left only one way to satisfy his curiosity before he continued on his way. He needed to spend more time with Bianca. That, he decided, was going to make this challenge even more interesting.

Chapter Five

"So what do you think of him?"

At Rosie's question, Bianca looked up from where she was fixing the sleeve of the gown she had been wearing the night Lucian stumbled into their house. She had not realized the ruffle at its hem had torn until she took it from her cupboard this morning.

The sunlight was glorious, and butterflies of almost every imaginable shade flitted through the kitchen garden. Through the trees, the sea was visible. Once again it was calm, its waves sliding up against the shore in an invitation to explore what awaited a traveler beyond the horizon.

"Ouch!" she exclaimed when she jabbed her finger with the needle. She should not have taken her attention away from her work. Popping her finger into her mouth, she said around it, "If you are speaking of Lucian—"

"Who else?"

"Mayhap Moss."

Rosie giggled as she glanced at the coachman, who was diligently rubbing Lucian's boots just outside the kitchen door. They already gleamed in the morning sunshine, but Moss must not have been satisfied because he was still buffing them with a rough cloth.

"Don't be silly!" Rosie wore a playful frown. "You know I was talking of *him*."

Bianca examined her finger, which gave her an excuse not to meet her sister's eyes. Rosie had taken to calling Lucian *him* because she could not bring herself to address an earl as Lucian, even though he had requested that all of them use his given name.

"What do you think of him?" Rosie asked.

"What do I think? I think Lucian will live. If I am not mistaken, I believe we will see him getting up and about as soon as Moss delivers those boots to him." She smiled as she realized the coachee must know that, too. That might explain why he was finishing the task with such meticulous and slow care. Every minute he delayed delivering the boots to Lucian was another that Lucian would rest.

"That is not what I meant."

"Then say what you mean. It is not like you to talk in riddles."

Setting the bowl of peas that she had shucked on the ground, Rosie stood. She sat next to Bianca on the bench in the kitchen garden. "I mean just what I said. I am interested in your opinion of *him*."

"Lucian has a great deal of Town polish, but he seems to be a pleasant enough chap." Her stomach twisted, for she was not being completely honest with her sister. Lucian's touch had created sensations she had never experienced, sensations that urged her to toss caution aside and explore each one with him. She would be a fool to do so.

"Is that all you can say?"

"He is well-favored, and he has a honed wit that I had not expected in a London dandy." She did not pause as she asked, "And what do *you* think of him?"

"I think he tells the funniest stories." Rosie put her fingers to her lips as another giggle escaped. "I particularly liked the one about the man who got so foxed that he fell asleep in the middle of the floor at Almack's."

"I did not hear that one."

"It was when you were making tea for us yesterday." Rosie hesitated, then said, "I believe Aunt Millicent has come to see that he is not a rake because she let you remain alone with him for a few minutes last evening."

Bianca laughed. "I would not agree with that, because Lucian may be the greatest rogue in England. We have seen him only when he has been left feeble by his fever. Even so, he seems to have charmed Aunt Millicent."

"He is very charming."

"Has he charmed you, too?" Bianca was not surprised when her sister now would not meet her eyes.

Rosie rubbed her hands together. "As I said, he is very charming. I think he could charm any woman he met."

Any woman? Bianca bit her lip as inspiration burst through her head. In just minutes after they met, Lucian had drawn Rosie out from behind her wall of shyness. He had done it without lathering her with false compliments. Although Rosie's smile remained bashful in his company, she did not stare again at the floor as she usually did when a stranger entered their home. Rosie was beautiful, and Lucian was an earl who, Moss had been quick to inform them, was without a wife to give him an heir.

Rosie and Lucian could be the perfect match. That Rosie was talking about him was proof that she was intrigued with him as she had never been about another man. All Bianca needed to do was find ways to bring them together. She would also have to avoid any opportunity that brought her close to Lucian again. She must not let him captivate her with his touch, which put strange ideas in her head and created those feelings she could not control. Being out of control was a most alien sensation, and she did not like it.

Making a match for her sister was a wonderful idea, for she feared Rosie would not consider any suitor until Bianca was wed. Bianca had no interest in marrying now because she had a promise to fulfill in honor of their late brother. Only when she did as she had vowed could she consider her own future, but the vow did not preclude her from finding Rosie a match.

As her sister, singing a lighthearted tune, took the peas into the house to be cooked for their evening meal, Bianca leaned back on the bench and smiled. A match between an earl and a baron's daughter was not impossible. Bianca needed to find a way to make it possible without letting herself be enticed again by Lucian. It would not be an easy task, but it was one she believed she could accomplish.

Aunt Millicent slammed the front door behind her so hard that Bianca rushed out of the parlor to see what was amiss.

"That man is being brought to Plymouth harbor," her aunt replied.

Bianca instantly knew whom Aunt Millicent was

furious about: Napoleon Bonaparte. For more than a month, the erstwhile emperor had been in English custody while his enemies in England and on the Continent tried to decide what to do with him.

Her hands clenched. He was a prisoner, but he was being treated with all the deference due to an emperor. So many people had died because of his yearning to hold dominion over Europe. So many, including her brother.

"Why is the government taking him to Plymouth?" She shuddered as though something disgusting were crawling along her skin. The ship would pass right by their cottage, but she doubted they would see it from shore. That would not keep her from watching for it. She was unsure what good would come from standing on the shore and staring out into the sea for a single ship, but she had promised herself that Napoleon should not go into exile without knowing the cost of his imperial dreams.

Aunt Millicent patted Bianca's hand as if the gentle motion would console both of them. "The vicar said they are taking him there while they are awaiting orders to sail with him to some distant island where he will be banished forever."

"We believed he was banished forever when he was imprisoned on Elba, and he escaped from there to begin the war anew."

"I cannot believe our leaders would allow him to escape a second time. They will guard him well until he can be sent to an island so remote there is no fear that he will return to try to claim the throne of France and the rest of Europe." She untied her bonnet and set it on its peg. As she walked with Bianca into the parlor, she said, "The vicar also mentioned that the ship he was on would be anchored not far from shore, so any final negotiations could be completed with ease."

Bianca's heart began pounding. Was it possible? Napoleon would be only two days' journey away and only a short distance off-shore from the city of Plymouth. It offered the chance she had long wished for. Since the news of Kevin's death, Bianca had started and thrown out numerous letters to that horrible Corsican. She had put her pain into each one, trying to express in words how Kevin's death had ripped apart their family in so many ways. She had promised Kevin that Napoleon would understand what suffering was.

Now she could tell Napoleon to his face!

She barely dared to believe that the vagaries of the government had brought her this chance. She imagined standing on the deck of his prison ship and telling Napoleon in her very best French how many lives had been destroyed by his dreams of an empire. She did not want to think about how she would gain permission to come aboard the ship. That was something she would worry about after she found a way to get to Plymouth. There must be some way. She would never have another opportunity to speak with Napoleon.

"You look pensive, Bianca," Aunt Millicent said.

"I am thinking of how glad I am that Napoleon soon will be on his way far from here." She sat on the settee, glad she did not have to lie to her aunt. She *would* be relieved when he was forgotten on his faraway island.

Her aunt sat beside her. "This justice is long overdue."

"Justice? There cannot be any true justice for a man who crowned himself emperor and reveled in war. Nothing can change what he did."

"I know."

Bianca leaned her head on her aunt's shoulder. "I miss Kevin so much."

"So do I."

"I try to get some comfort from knowing that serving in the army is what Kevin wanted to do." She sighed and then stood. "Forgive me for being maudlin. It makes me angry that Kevin is dead and Napoleon continues to negotiate with the British government. What does he want? He is lucky he is alive."

"He wishes to go to America," Lucian said as he came into the parlor.

Bianca stared as she heard her aunt's quick intake of breath. Lucian looked every inch an earl from the perfect cut of his navy blue coat to his waistcoat with its gold buttons and his light tan breeches that reached into his glistening boots. As he walked into the room, he took care not to brush his left arm against any furniture.

She had not realized that he had come down the stairs. Seeing Moss behind him on the stairs, she knew the coachman could not have delayed further in delivering Lucian's boots to him.

Again she looked at Lucian. She had not guessed he was so tall, for when they stood side-by-side his head was almost the same height as gangly Moss's. It no longer seemed far-fetched to believe Rosie's exclamation that the earl from Bianca's fairy tale had emerged from the story to enter their lives. Her pulse pounded in her head like a team of runaway horses, fast and perilous.

His eyes swept the room, and she was aware of how threadbare it would appear compared to the magnificent houses he was accustomed to. Although they had been allowed to bring a few pieces with them from Dunsworthy Hall, most of the furnishings were worn.

Then his gaze locked with hers, and everything melted away but the powerful emotions within them. She longed to look away before he discovered every secret within her soul, but she could not. He raised his hand. Her fingers settled on his palm. He bowed over her hand, not releasing her gaze.

"America?" asked Aunt Millicent as Moss went out the front door.

Bianca hastily looked away from Lucian's compelling eyes. She did not glance in her aunt's direction, for she suspected her face was branded with the heat from those eyes. Her cheeks were hot enough to be as scarlet as a flame.

"Why America?" her aunt continued.

Lucian started to shrug, then halted with a wince. "Mayhap he believes the Americans will recall the debt they owe the French for their help during their War of Independence."

"But the Americans declared war on France and Napoleon, too," Bianca said.

"I am sure Napoleon has admirers and friends who have created several schemes on his behalf." He smiled. "Do not worry, Bianca."

"I am not worried." She looked at him again.

When his smile widened and his eyes led hers toward where he still held her hand, she said, "Sit down here, Lucian. You should make haste with care."

"I have learned that, but I cannot sit when two lovely ladies are on their feet."

Aunt Millicent motioned for Bianca to sit as she did so herself.

Bianca drew Lucian toward a chair. He moved toward her as gracefully as if music played through the room. She half-expected him to twirl her about in the steps of a country dance, but releasing her hand, he sat. She perched on the edge of another chair as she folded her hands in her lap. Had he felt how her fingers trembled when he held them? She guessed he had, for he seemed aware of too much.

Had she lost her mind? She was supposed to be devising a way to persuade him to consider a match with Rosie. Letting thoughts of him and his bold touch linger in her mind would get in the way of those plans.

"Do not look so distressed, Bianca," he said, and she dared to hope he had misread her reactions. "I doubt Boney's request will be considered seriously by the government. Even America is not far enough away for that serpent."

Aunt Millicent said quietly, "This time, I believe wiser heads will prevail, and he will be sent where he cannot bother anyone again." With a smile, she said, "You look much better, Lucian."

"I feel much better. Rosie's cooking seems to be having a great and wondrous effect on my health."

"Rosie's cooking and Bianca's care of your wound." Aunt Millicent's smile became more sincere. "They are an amazing duo."

"I would agree." He looked at Bianca. "Some fresh air would be invigorating. Would you join me for a walk along the shore?"

"You are barely out of bed," Bianca replied, aghast. "Do you think you should exert yourself so?"

"Yes."

She laughed at his emphatic answer. Almost two weeks had passed since he had arrived at Dunsworthy Dower Cottage. In the past few days, when she had passed his open door on the upper floor, she had seen him looking out like a forlorn child. Aunt Millicent had strictly forbidden him to leave his bed until he had been without any sign of fever or infection for three days.

"I will go with you for a walk," she said, "as long as we do not walk too far. I do not want to have to send for Moss to tote you home if you overdo. Aunt Millicent, would you like to join us?"

"No, no," her aunt replied, patting her shoulder. "I will stay here and wait for Rosie to come back from her call on Mrs. Nichols." To Lucian, she added, "Mrs. Nichols and Rosie have been bosom-bows since they were very young. Now Mrs. Nichols has a new baby, and Rosie has been eager to see the little boy."

"Rosie loves children," Bianca hurried to say, looking sideways at Lucian, so he would not guess she had an ulterior reason for praising her sister. "They love her, too. You will see if you join us at the summer festival in the village this Saturday."

"Summer festival? What sort of festival?"

Aunt Millicent shooed them toward the door. "If you want to get some fresh air before tea, you need to go now." She wagged a finger at him. "Do not be jobbernowl and do too much!"

He bowed his head to her. "You have my word on

it, and I can assure you that a Wandersee's word is always kept."

"I will see that he does not overexert himself," Bianca added while she tied her bonnet ribbons. She would not let a moment of this walk be cut short, because here was the chance to begin her plan to convince him that Rosie would be the perfect bride for him. She could praise Rosie whenever possible, taking care not to be obvious in what she was doing.

"See that you do make sure he takes care." Aunt Millicent closed the door behind them.

"This way," Bianca said, motioning toward the trees at the end of a short path. "There is a way through the trees that leads down to the beach." She bent and petted Barley on the head as the large dog leaped toward them then away through the trees, obviously delighted to have someone to share his romp.

"On the other side of the road to Plymouth?"

Her steps faltered. "Plymouth? Are you bound for Plymouth?"

"Yes."

"I had no idea," she said to hide her astonishment that he would be going in the same direction as Napoleon. She shook that thought from her head. Many people traveled to Plymouth. Moss had said Lucian was going to call on friends, a journey that must have been planned before the announcement was made that Napoleon was being taken there.

"Why should you?" His reasonable tone irked her.

"You have talked about so many other things," she retorted. "I find it odd that you never mentioned your destination."

His brows lowered. "Is there something wrong with my destination? You look so pale that one would guess you thought a murderer was beyond those trees and ready to jump out and attack you."

A murderer might now be just beyond the trees, if Napoleon's ship was sailing past while they spoke. Suddenly another burst of inspiration filled her head.

"Bianca," he asked again, "is something wrong?"

Nothing was wrong. Everything was remarkably right about his destination, if she could persuade him to make it her destination as well. She could not believe how everything was coming together to give her the opportunity she craved. Two opportunities, in fact, because her new idea was as perfect as the one of making Rosie his bride. Not only did she want to keep the promise she had made to Kevin's memory, but Lucian needed to be longer in the company of shy Rosie if there was to be any hope of a match.

Taking care not to give a hint of her thoughts, she said, "I have heard much about the city of Plymouth, although I have never been there."

"As you know, I am going to visit a friend. He is about to walk quite willingly into the parson's mouse-trap."

"Mouse-trap?"

He smiled. "He is about to be married, poor chap."

"You make marriage sound like a horrible state."

"It can be, if a man does not consider what it means."

"The same could be said for a woman," she shot back, then wished she had not. She wanted to talk about a marriage between him and Rosie.

With a chuckle, he drew in a deep breath. "Ah, the flavor of salt in the air. It is one of the finest flavors in the world."

"I am accustomed to it. I no longer take time to savor it."

"Then do so." He paused as they emerged from the trees' shadows. Putting his hands to his chest, he said, "Take a deep breath and enjoy it." He pulled in one of his own. "Go ahead."

She did. When he urged her to release it slowly, relishing every bit of its zest, she could not keep from laughing.

"Don't choke on it," he said with a laugh. He took her hand and stroked it as his smile grew warm.

Or was it she who was growing warm? Gazing down at his fingers upon her skin, she marveled at how such a simple touch could create such an explosion of sensation within her. Her other hand was smoothing his hair back from his eyes before she had time to think about the complications a simple touch could create.

Bianca pulled back her fingers and clasped her hands in front of her. She was supposed to be arranging for him to fall in love with Rosie. Looking out at the undulating waves, she said, "I had forgotten how wondrous the sea air is."

"You must not forget again. I love the sea and its temperament, both good and bad." He followed her toward the path to the shore, and she was glad he did not offer his arm. She did not want to insult him, but touching him again would be perilous to her plan. "I have long wondered if my family's name did not come from a desire to travel far across the waves."

"Take care," she said as they began down the path edging the low cliffs. When Barley bolted past them, barking and scattering the sea birds, she added, "Do not take your cue from Barley. This path is steeper than the one we will use to go back up to the road. If you fall, you could reinjure your arm."

"Along with other parts of me." He leaned toward her. "Of course, I would have you to bind up my wounds and watch over me, wouldn't I?"

"You are assuming much." She edged away from him and skipped the rest of the way down to the shore, which was interspersed with sand and rocks of every size. Looking back at him, she said, "I have tended all the wounds I wish to for you, Lucian. Both for your sake and mine."

His face became abruptly serious as he walked toward where she stood. "I appreciate your kindness, Bianca. I owe you a duty that I hope someday I may repay."

"If you repay it now, you will not have the weight of that debt upon you."

He smiled. "You *are* always forthright, aren't you?"

"Always." She grinned back at him. "I have found it saves a great deal of time to be frank."

He did not answer as they strolled along the shore. The sea whispered against the beach, and the breeze was gentle. Bright sunshine burned through Bianca's straw poke bonnet.

Barley raced past them again, barking at something she had not seen. His paws raised a cloud of sand. Some sifted into her shoes. Standing on one foot, she drew off her slipper and shook the sand from it.

"You look like a crane," Lucian said with a chuckle.

She raised her head. That was foolish, she discovered as she wobbled. Lucian put his hand on her shoulder. To steady her, she assumed, but the heat that flowed through her threatened to turn her knees to jam. She sat with a graceless thump on the sand.

He laughed hard and with more vigor than she had heard before. Holding out his hand, he asked, "Would you like help up?"

"Your help landed me here."

"Quite to the contrary. I tried to keep you from falling." He knelt on one knee beside her. "You folded up like Andover did when I gave him a facer."

"The man who shot you?"

He nodded. "It was not very sporting of me to give him a plumper to the face."

"A what?"

"Plumper. A blow to the face which usually causes it to puff up."

"That is a grotesque term!" She frowned. "And fisticuffs are equally grotesque."

"Not as grotesque as shooting a man because you believed quite wrongly he was dallying with your mistress."

Bianca pulled on her slipper and stood. "I doubt I shall ever comprehend the peculiar ways of the *ton*."

"Your aunt does." He came to his feet. "Did she have a Season in London?"

"She was there for part of one, but came to take care of us when my parents died. We were quite young, and, as our father's sister, she assumed the responsibility for us."

He moved toward the water's edge, where the waves darkened the sand and rocks. "I cannot believe that a woman with her kind heart and obvious beauty did not find a match in short order."

"My father's gambling habits left nothing for her dowry."

"Or yours."

Bianca clamped her lips closed before she could reply that she was worried only about a dowry for Rosie. Playing the matchmaker required that Lucian not guess he was being steered to see that Rosie was the perfect bride for him.

Quietly, she said, "I should not have spoken of such things to you. Rosie tells me often that I should think before I speak. She has that ability to restrain her words, but I do not seem to be able to master it."

"Are you saying you should not have spoken of your father's habits because I am a stranger?"

"Hardly, for you have been at our house for nearly a fortnight now, and you must own that you have had more attention paid to you than the customary guest would receive."

He tucked her hand into his right arm without a pause in his steps. She had to skip half a pace to compensate for his longer ones, for he did not slow down. She hoped he was not planning to try to catch up with Barley, who was halfway to where the cove curved back upon itself.

"There is no question that I owe you a duty for saving my life, which I nearly threw away with my own stupidity," he said.

"But you mentioned that you had to fight that duel to save a friend's life."

"I suspect there would have been other ways to deal with Andover, if I had been thinking more clearly." He grinned. "I seldom do my best thinking when a gun is pressed to my back."

"Oh, I had no idea!" She regarded him with astonishment. That he had survived such an encounter was a tribute to his calm head.

"In addition, there is that small matter of me blackening your eye."

She touched her cheek. "It has almost faded."

"Into a hideous shade of green."

"Thank you for the compliment, my lord."

He bowed to her as he had to her aunt. "If you choose always to be frank, I shall be the same. It is a refreshing change from the carefully composed words of the Polite World. So let me be straightforward and ask you what duty I can do for you that will even the scale."

"Take us with you to Plymouth after the summer festival in the village."

"Why do you want to go to Plymouth?" His lips tipped in a wry smile. "Do you have a lover there with the navy?"

She stopped and folded her arms in front of her. How could he alter from pleasant to vexing in the midst of a single sentence? "Do not be boorish, and please do not speak so when Rosie is near. She is a far gentler soul than I am."

"So you do not have a lover?"

"Even if I were to answer that, I would be likely to ask you the same question. Of course, you would take great glee in regaling me with a long list of names."

"I *am* a gentleman, Bianca."

"A gentleman would not have asked such a question of me in the first place."

He drew her hand to his arm again. "I profess to a great curiosity about why you would ask this of a near stranger—and I know that we have seen a great deal of each other in the past few days, but you do not know me nor do I know you. I do not know if you like red roses better or white ones."

"White," she answered, walking rapidly again to keep up with him. "Rosie prefers red ones."

"Nor do I know if you prefer iced or uniced cakes with your tea."

"Iced, without question. Rosie agrees with me on that topic."

His eyes narrowed at the mention of her sister's name again. She must take care that he not suspect the truth of why she kept speaking of Rosie. "Nor do I—"

"Lucian," she said with impatience for they were almost to the other path that led up toward the road, "I have seen you are a trustworthy man."

He laughed. "That is your first error in assuming you know me. I doubt I could be deemed trustworthy when alone with a lovely woman."

"But, other than your single comment, you have been the epitome of a gentleman."

"How could I even consider acting otherwise? I knew your aunt had set Moss to watch us." He pointed up toward the rim of the hill.

Bianca saw a quick motion, but that was enough to show her that he was right. Moss was trying to keep out of view while still keeping them in his sights. "Be that as it may, I am asking you to take me to Plymouth."

"Be that as it may," he replied back in the same taut tone, "I am puzzled why you would ask me, a near stranger, to let you travel with me to Plymouth."

"Not just me, but Rosie and Aunt Millicent."

"You want me to escort all of you to Plymouth?"

"Yes."

Lucian fought not to laugh at Bianca's easy confidence that he would agree to her request without protest. "And I assume you wish me to escort you back here as well?"

"Yes, although I would not impose on you to go out of your way to return us here. You could offer us the use of your carriage to make our trip back to Dunsworthy Dower Cottage."

He cursed under his breath. This woman had too dashedly a lively wit, for she always had an answer for anything he said. "You still have not answered my question. Why do you wish to go to Plymouth rather than to London or Brighton or Bath?"

"I could say it is because that is where you are bound."

His roar of laughter startled Barley, who ran back to where they stood and began to bark. Ignoring the dog, he said, "Your attempt at a feigned affection is futile, Bianca. It might have worked if—"

"If I had batted my eyelashes at you like a coquette?"

"Mayhap." He grasped her elbow. Turning her to face him, he saw her astonishment. "Or it might have been more convincing if you had done this." He took her hand and lifted it to his shoulder. When she drew her hand back, he caught it again and pinned it against his chest. "Even this might have persuaded me."

"Will you stop?"

"When you tell me why you want to go to Plymouth." He raised a single finger between them, still holding her hand beneath his other hand. "The truth, Bianca."

"The truth is my business."

"Not if I am escorting you there. If you are planning some sort of mischief, then I could be implicated in the muddle that is sure to ensue."

She lowered her eyes. "I am planning no mischief, I assure you."

"Then why do you wish to go there?" He put his bent finger beneath her chin and tipped it up. When her gaze met his, he said, "The truth, Bianca."

She stared up at him, and he resisted the enticement of her blue-gray eyes. They were incredible eyes, darker on the edge of the color and then softening within. Quite the opposite of the woman herself, he suspected. Or was he making a mistake? Was she as gentle inside as her sister Rosie was outwardly?

"You want the truth?" she asked.

"That is what I said."

"Remember that you asked." She gave him a cool smile, and he steeled himself for what she was about to say. Even as little as he knew of Bianca Dunsworthy, he knew that he would be a fool to think he could guess what was in her mind when she wore that smile.

"I shall," he replied.

"I want to see the ship where Napoleon is imprisoned."

"What?" He took a step back from her and regarded her with confusion. He had thought she was the most practical woman he had ever met, but now she was making this want-witted request.

"I want to see where the man who caused so many deaths is imprisoned." Tears filled her eyes, causing him to wonder for whom she still mourned, but they did not fall along her cheeks. "Will you take me and Rosie and Aunt Millicent to Plymouth with you?"

He could not be unmoved by her brave battle

against her own grief. Nor could he fail to notice his own reaction of regret at those tears. He had been teasing her about a lover, not guessing how cruel his words might be. If she had lost the man she loved in the maw of Napoleon's well-trained army, how could he deny her this chance to heal her heart by allowing her to see how low Boney had fallen?

There had been more than regret in his reaction to her request. There had been . . . envy. He did not want to feel that emotion, but the cramp in his gut stank surprisingly of envy. Was he out of his mind? Even with the low situation she had found herself in as the daughter of a spendthrift baron, she was a beautiful woman. She may have had many suitors, and she might have many more after he did her this one small favor.

"Yes," he heard himself saying before he had time to consider what a jumble he was about to make of his life. When she whispered her thanks, he knew he could not take back his offer. But he suspected he was going to wish often that he had.

Chapter Six

"Bianca tells me you are quite fond of red roses," Lucian said as he paused by the gate to the cottage. A lush rosebush was draped over the stones. "Did you plant these, Rosie?"

"No."

"A silly question, for I can see, upon closer examination, this bush must have been here for many years before you were born. I trust you will forgive my question." He laughed even though he did not feel like it. The sound was flat, and he wished he had not tried to leaven the conversation with some humor.

"Yes," Rosie said in hardly more than a whisper.

He reached to open the gate for her. A twinge flitted across his left shoulder, but he paid it no mind. It was less troublesome than his fruitless attempts to draw more than a single word at a time out of Rosie. Even those words had been reluctant.

"Thank you," she murmured as she slipped past him.

He closed the gate after him and stepped around some chickens in the yard. "And I thank you for going on this walk with me. Your aunt tells me the fresh air will be good for my recovery."

"Yes." She opened the kitchen **door** and stepped inside. "Thank you."

Lucian waited until the kitchen door had closed behind Rosie before he turned toward the stable. If he did not know about her shyness, he would guess she despised him. Questions about the festival in the village of Dunstanbury had not even brought much of a response, although he could tell by her bashful smile that she was looking forward to the gathering.

She was not so reserved when with her aunt and sister. He had heard Rosie sing as they worked together in the kitchen, and it was a bright and lyrical sound. And it vanished whenever he was near.

So why had he gone for a stroll with her? He had not even intended to take a walk with Rosie this morning. Being alone with his thoughts while he stepped quickly along the shore path to regain his strength had been his plan. Yet, somehow, when he left the cottage, Rosie had been with him.

Recreating the conversation just before he left, he was startled to recall that it had been *Bianca* who had suggested that Rosie go with him. Her sister had been hesitant about accompanying him until *Bianca* offered the idea of going no farther than the field that separated the cottage from Dunsworthy Hall. *Bianca* had soothed her sister's concerns by saying that Moss would be working outside the stable, and Lucian and Rosie never would wander out of the coachee's view. *Bianca* had offered to get her sister's bonnet, so Lucian was not delayed on his walk.

Bianca! By Jove, she had manipulated both him and Rosie. In retrospect, it was quite clear. And after stating that she was always frank.

"You look pensive," Moss said as he polished a piece of harness.

"Vexed is closer to the truth." Lucian rested one elbow on the fence that rose above the stone wall surrounding the stableyard.

"At Miss Rosie?"

"Other than to wonder if she will ever speak more than two words in a row to anyone other than her sister and aunt, who could ever be upset at that bashful girl?"

Moss chuckled. "She is not a girl, but a woman, and a woman has a way of getting a man vexed on his way to reeling him in to be her husband."

"You know a dashed lot about women for a man who has never married."

"Now you know why I never married."

Lucian smiled and looked back at the cottage with its thatched roof and the trees protecting it from the sea winds. "'Tis not Rosie who has vexed me, even though I am frustrated with my every attempt to have a conversation with her."

"She is a very reserved young woman." He looked up from the harness and added, "Some man will come along who knows how to draw her out of that shyness."

"And obviously I will not be the one."

"So if Miss Rosie is not vexing you, and as Miss Dunsworthy has come to treat you like a long-lost brother, it must be Miss Bianca who has exasperated you."

"She is an exasperating woman."

"The best ones are."

Lucian laughed and sat on a block of wood beside his coachee. Slipping off his coat and hanging it over the fence, he picked up another length of the reins and a cloth and went to work. "Again I am in awe of your knowledge of women."

"I would be glad to share what little I know."

"What are you waiting for, man? Tell me posthaste."

Moss paused in his task and smiled. "Everything I know about women can be stated in one sentence: we are not meant to understand them, just to appreciate them."

"Bah! I thought you had some wondrous secret you could share."

With a laugh, Moss bent to his work again. "If I knew everything there is to know about dealing with women, I would be hailed by every man as worthy of being crowned king. And I am not the king, so I will stick with my job as coachman and my very happy state of bachelorhood."

" 'Tis a state I intend to maintain now, too."

"Then take care, my lord, and heed the words of a man older than you. Getting you vexed is just the first step in a woman's scheme. Soon you will find she rouses you in other ways that have nothing to do with vexation."

"*That* I know." He rubbed the leather. "And I know, as well, how to avoid such a trap."

Moss glanced at him and merely raised his graying eyebrows. Even though the coachee said nothing, his expression was an eloquent, "Good luck."

With a chuckle, Lucian continued his work. Now that he was wise to Bianca's little game of match-making, he would say that *she* was the one in need of good fortune.

* * *

Bianca gazed through the carriage door in delight. She had never seen Dunstanbury look so beautiful. The Tudor fronts on the shops glistened in the bright sunshine, for the festival day had dawned with barely a cloud ruining the perfect palette of blue sky. The village was bedecked with flowers. Bushes were in bloom, and pots were set on every step. Barrows and wagons were set in the middle of the road and were overflowing with more blossoms. Scents from roses wafted on the air to season every breath.

People were already gathered on the small green set between the two sides of the village's only street. She saw a brightly painted red and blue wagon at the far end of the green. Every year, in spite of the village leaders' attempts to keep them away, gypsies took advantage of the festival to earn some money.

"Do you want to go to the festival or just admire it from here in the carriage?" asked Lucian as he held up his hand with obvious impatience.

She put her hand on his, but frowned. Since the beginning of the week when he had gone for a walk with Rosie, Lucian had been brusque with her. She had been secretly glad, because that gave Rosie more of a chance to sit with him, and Bianca made certain that her sister took advantage of every opportunity to do so. Yet, it was tiresome to have him act toward her as if she were too common even to be noticed by an earl.

"Thank you," Bianca said when she stepped to the ground and quickly released his hand before her fingers teased her into leaving them on his. She would not let her manners become tarnished simply because his had, and she must never forget her plan to show him that he would be wise to take Rosie as his bride.

But there was nothing improper about the way he

handed her sister and aunt out of the carriage. Bianca saw her sister take deep breaths and wondered if something was wrong or if Rosie was merely savoring the myriad scents of the festival. When Lucian offered his arm to Aunt Millicent, her aunt seemed astonished, but put her hand on it and walked with him toward the nearest shop.

Rosie glanced at Bianca, then quickly away. What was he thinking? He should have offered his arm to Rosie. After all, Rosie looked exceptionally lovely today in her pale ivory gown that made her red hair even more vibrant. Bianca had sewn a new flower onto her sister's straw bonnet, and it gave a perky bounce with each step Rosie took. Her own dress was a green that was nearly the color of the grass, and her bonnet had no decoration. Today was supposed to be Rosie's day to catch Lucian's eye once and for all while Bianca blended in with the greenery.

It was the perfect step in the plan to persuade Lucian that he should consider courting and marrying Rosie. Only two things had gone wrong. Bianca had not considered that he would ask Aunt Millicent to let him escort her to look at the flowers. Nor had she guessed how a pinch of some strange emotion would torment her each time she glanced at where Aunt Millicent and Lucian were talking together, their lighthearted laughter reaching back to the carriage.

"Look there!" Rosie gasped, her voice dropping to a whisper as she grabbed Bianca's arm.

"Where?"

"There." She did not point to the right, but looked that way.

Bianca followed her sister's eyes. A man was emerging from a carriage as luxurious as Lucian's.

He was no stranger. He had black hair, an extraordinary color for the Dunsworthy family, which usually had red or blond hair. He was tall and possessed the same arrogant air of authority that Lucian had been exhibiting far too often in the past few days.

"What are you in a botheration about?" Bianca asked. "You knew Lord Dunsworthy would be here. Don't you remember? Aunt Millicent always made certain that Kevin attended, because the villagers like to have Lord Dunsworthy be present during the festival."

"He makes me sad."

Putting her arm around Rosie's shoulders, Bianca squeezed them gently. "You cannot blame Lord Dunsworthy for Kevin's death."

"But it is not fair that Kevin is not here to enjoy this day. He loved to come to the festival, and he should be here now."

"No, it is not fair that he is not here, but that is the way it has turned out." She looked toward the west and Plymouth so her sister would not see the tears flooding her eyes. "At least now we can hope that justice will be served when Napoleon is sent to his island prison for the rest of his life."

Rosie wrung her hands, not willing to be distracted from her despair. "Do we need to speak with Lord Dunsworthy? I swear, Bianca, I will cry if I have to."

"You will not cry, and you do not need to speak with him, but you must come with me while I go to speak with him."

"Isn't that one and same?"

"Mayhap, but he is part of our family, and we owe him a greeting."

Walking toward Lord Dunsworthy, Bianca linked her arm through her sister's. She did not think that Rosie would turn and run, but she wanted to make certain her sister was by her side. Bianca kept her head high, because she feared tears would flood out of her own eyes. This man, through no fault of his own, save his birth, was a constant reminder of their loss.

"Good day, cousin," she said when they paused by the carriage they once had ridden in. A man she did not know was sitting in the box, and she wondered if the new Lord Dunsworthy had brought his own household with him. She had not heard of anyone being let go, so Allen Dunsworthy must have a large fortune to continue to pay so many employees.

"Ah, Primrose," he replied.

"No, I am Bianca." She looked at her sister and gave her a smile that ordered Rosie to smile, too, instead of appearing positively stricken with grief. "My sister is Primrose."

The baron laughed. "I am not good at all with names. I would forget my own, I swear, if—Wandersee, what are you doing here?"

Bianca stiffened at the baron's greeting, which proved he was not as poor with names as he averred. Then, she realized, he might be as uncomfortable with this situation as she and Rosie—and Aunt Millicent—were.

Lucian paused next to her and shook the baron's hand. "I made an unscheduled stop in your little village. Miss Dunsworthy and her nieces have been my hosts, and they insisted that I join them here today for your festival."

"This festival? Why are you interested in this silly day?" Lord Dunsworthy asked. "It is not as if you have a duty to be here."

Bianca noticed several of the townsfolk in earshot

bristling at how the new baron belittled this festival. It had been held in Dunstanbury for so long that no one even remembered why it had been started, other than as a break from the long hours of tending the summer fields.

"I cannot tell you why I am interested," Lucian answered smoothly, "for I have only just arrived, and I have yet to see all there is to see."

"Is that your carriage?"

"Yes."

"I knew a carriage that fine did not belong to anyone who lived nearby." Lord Dunsworthy motioned toward the green. "Allow me, Wandersee, to show you what little there is to see."

"Of course." Lucian bowed his head toward Bianca and her sister and aunt. "If you will be so kind as to excuse us, ladies."

"Of course." Bianca did not lower her eyes, even when she saw amusement in Lucian's at how she copied Lord Dunsworthy's obsequious tone. Turning her back on them as if the two men had already walked away, she asked in a much lighter voice, "Where would you like to go first? *We* know how much fun there is to be found today."

Aunt Millicent wore an expression of dismay, and Bianca was instantly contrite. She did not want to upset her aunt any further. Yet she needed to show that she did not care if the two men, who had acted as if the three of them had vanished, chose to ignore them. Her exasperation now focused on her cousin. It seemed as if everyone was conspiring to keep Lucian and Rosie apart today. Wanting to ask her aunt to forgive her thoughtless action, she said nothing. She could not be sure what might be overheard and reach the new Lord Dunsworthy's ear. Or worse, Lucian's.

Her aunt's smile returned as they went from barrow to barrow to admire the wealth of flowers in dozens of shades. Each household vied to have the most fragrant flowers blooming on festival day. Music came from a platform set in front of the church, and there would be dancing later.

That thought dismissed Bianca's regret. Dancing would mean another opportunity for Lucian to take notice of her sister. Imagining him asking Rosie to dance and Rosie agreeing added a cheerful bounce to her steps. If she had been wearing a flower like Rosie's, it would have been in danger of being jostled right off. It was going to be a good day, after all.

Bianca applauded along with the rest of the crowd gathered in front of the church as the children's chorus completed another song. The vicar had been working with the youngsters for the past month to learn the lyrics and melodies so they could entertain today. She smiled as she recalled how she and her siblings had attended the practices and stood in those uneven rows when they were young enough to be in the chorus. It seemed almost like someone else's life now when Kevin was not with them. She shook away the thought. Her brother would hate her maudlin thoughts, for he always had teased her out of her dismals. His pranks always left her laughing so hard she forgot what had distressed her.

"You must be enjoying yourself," Lucian said as he sat next to her on the blanket spread out beneath a tree. "I have never seen such a happy smile on your face."

"Just remembering when Rosie and Kevin and I were part of that chorus."

"Who is Kevin?"

She stared at him, astonished. How could he have been in Dunsworthy Dower Cottage for so long and not know about Kevin? Aunt Millicent and Rosie seldom spoke of him, but she knew he was in their thoughts as he was in hers.

"My brother," she answered quietly.

"Your brother?" He paused as the vicar introduced the next song, then asked, "Why have you never mentioned him before?"

"I thought I had."

"No."

As the childish voices washed over her, she said, "Kevin was killed on the Continent, and our cousin Allen became Lord Dunsworthy in his place."

"I had no idea." He looked toward where the crenellated walls of Dunsworthy Hall were visible in the distance. "That is why you and your sister and your aunt live in the dower cottage."

"Yes. Aunt Millicent thought it would be simpler for everyone that way."

"Has it been?"

She faltered, not sure how to answer the question that no one else had asked; not even she had asked it. She decided to be honest. "How can I know if it has been simpler or not? My life has taken this turn, so I cannot be privy to what it would have been if Kevin were still alive."

"You and your sister would be the talk of the *ton*."

When a laugh escaped from her, she put her hand over her mouth as those standing and sitting nearby gave her angry glances. She must not interrupt the choir's song.

"What is so funny?" Lucian asked.

"I fear you are correct, although I doubt Rosie and I would have been the talk of the *ton* in the complimentary way I assume you meant. No doubt I would have said the wrong thing to the wrong person at the very worst moment and been banned from any other events in the Polite World for the rest of my life."

"I find that hard to believe." He leaned toward her, his eyes sparkling with merriment. She noticed that, as always, he had sat down on her right, so there would be no chance of him reinjuring his arm. Although he tried to hide that it bothered him, she had seen him wince several times each day since he had left his sickbed. "In fact, I'm willing to wager that you could last a whole weekend without saying the wrong thing to the wrong person at the very worst moment and end up being ostracized by the Polite World."

"A wager is easy to make when there is no way to prove it."

"But there is." He toyed with the ribbon on her bonnet, his finger stroking her cheek so lightly that she did not dare to react, for the sweet warmth might vanish. "You could join me at my friend's gathering in Plymouth. You would have plenty of chances to win the wager by embarrassing yourself in front of the *ton*."

Bianca turned away from his dynamic eyes, relieved for the excuse. She clapped as the children finished their fourth song. There would be one more, because the vicar always had them sing five songs. The last one would be a hymn.

"Well?" Lucian asked when the children began

singing again, more enthusiastically because the hymn was familiar.

"Hush. I want to listen to the song."

"Afraid to accept my invitation and wager?"

"No, I like this song. Hush!"

The applause was exuberant when the children finished the last note. It was, as it was every year, a bit off-key, but no one seemed to notice. As the children raced off to play on the green, Aunt Millicent waved from near the church's porch.

Bianca stood. "I need to find out what my aunt wants."

"She is probably curious why your face is nearly as red as Rosie's hair."

"I am not blushing."

"No?" He took her hand and put it against her cheek.

She was amazed to feel how hot her face was. Not from embarrassment, she knew, because she had not done or said anything to cause her to flush crimson. As his fingers uncurled to rest atop hers on her cheek, she could not deny the truth. Lucian was causing this heat. Not him, she tried to argue with herself, but his offer to be part of the *ton* for an elegant party. It was an exciting idea and far beyond anything she had conceived, other than when she was making up a story for Rosie and Aunt Millicent to enjoy.

"Lucian," she said quietly, "I cannot keep Aunt Millicent waiting."

"You are making me wait."

"For what?"

"An answer to my invitation."

Aunt Millicent waved faster.

"I must go," Bianca said. "We can talk about this later."

"I shall not forget it."

Nor shall I. She was glad she had not let those words slip from her mouth as she hurried across the green, easing through the crowd of people gathering for the dancing that always followed the chorus's performance.

Aunt Millicent grasped Bianca's hands, but she looked past her, and Bianca knew Lucian had followed her. Her burst of irritation became gratitude that he was here when her aunt said, "I cannot find Rosie."

"Cannot find her?" Lucian repeated, his smile disappearing. He had never seen Millicent Dunsworthy so unsettled. "Are you saying that she is missing?"

"I fear so." Millicent took a shuddering breath. "I was speaking with one of my friends, and she became bored with the conversation and took off. I do not know where, but I have been searching for her since the children started singing. It is not like her to miss that."

He scanned the crowd, looking for the silly flower Rosie wore on her bonnet today. He did not see it. "You two check the shops, and I will look around the green here. We will meet at the blanket by the tree where you were sitting, Bianca." Letting his hand linger on Bianca's shoulder for only a moment, he smiled. "Do not fret."

"I will not. There is little to fear in such a small village." She glanced toward where her aunt was hurrying across the green. "Aunt Millicent worries too much about us sometimes."

"She does not want to lose another of you."

Bianca looked up at him, amazement widening her incredible eyes. He wondered what it would be like to dive into those depths that were the same color as the sea. Could a man drown in them, or would he find himself floating peacefully? No, there would be no peace with Bianca, for her fiery emotions made that impossible.

His fingers brushed her cheek, which had been ruddy moments ago and now was as white as the roses she loved. Much to his regret, her eyes closed for a moment. They reopened, and he felt his breath clog within him. He did not dare to release it, for even the slight motion might tear her gaze from his.

"I never thought of her concern that way," she whispered. "Dear Aunt Millicent, she worries about Rosie and me too much."

"I doubt she believes so."

"And she most likely believes as well that she has cause to worry about us." She smiled, and her eyes softened. "Me, most definitely."

Although he wanted to ask what mischief Bianca had caused that added to her aunt's fretting, Lucian said nothing as her aunt motioned for her to catch up.

Quickly, he discovered the idea of searching the green by himself had been optimistic. More people had arrived to enjoy the evening's food and entertainment. Half the countryside must be empty, as people poured into the village. He tried to protect his left arm, but it was bumped again and again. The search while he wandered about the green was fruitless. If he was going to make this worthwhile, he needed to retrace Rosie's steps since she had arrived at the festival.

He strode toward where the carriage had been left. Moss and Lord Dunsworthy's coachee would be two more sets of eyes to look for Rosie, and the baron's driver might know of others who could assist without causing an uproar. Even though he believed Millicent's fears were unfounded, for no criminal could pass unnoticed through the crowd on the green, he could understand how precious her nieces were to her.

Moss was sitting on the carriage step when Lucian reached him. The coachman jumped to his feet and put his finger to his lips.

Lucian smiled, suspecting he knew the answer before he asked, "Have you seen Miss Rosie?"

"Yes, my lord. She is sleeping in the carriage."

"Her aunt is distressed that Miss Rosie has gone missing." He chuckled softly when he saw the bonnet with its bright flower balanced on the seat across from where the young woman was napping.

"Do you wish me to wake her?"

He shook his head. "No need. While you continue to stand guard here, I will find Miss Dunsworthy and Miss Bianca to let them know she is safe. Thank you, Moss, for watching over her."

"I trust you are having a good time, my lord," Moss said before sitting on the step carefully so he would not jar the carriage.

"Yes, I am." Lucian grinned as he ducked back into the crowd, again holding his left arm close to him. He *was* having a good time, and he guessed it would only get better, because he had been honest with Bianca. He would not let her forget his invitation to Jordan's gathering. If she accepted, then it was time to put his own plan into place to show her the perils of matchmaking. If she refused his invitation, he would simply need to show her now. He knew, he realized with a rather wicked smile, just the way to do that.

Chapter Seven

Lanterns hung from the trees edging the green, looking as if giant glowworms had come to roost in them. Laughter and music combined to overwhelm conversation. The aromas of the food served two hours ago lingered in the air as the sun edged toward the western horizon. Although the sun was setting earlier tonight than it had on Midsummer's Day, it was past the time when most of the villagers sought their beds each night. Tonight, no one, save the babes, would get to sleep until past midnight.

Bianca walked aimlessly with her sister through the crowd. They paused and chatted with a friend, then moved on. This was not a night for long conversations, but for merriment and laughter shared with everyone.

"What a lovely day! I cannot wait for this festival to arrive each year," Rosie said as she swung her bonnet like a basket. "I swear I did not sleep a moment last night after you finished adding ruffles to my gown."

"Which is why you fell asleep in the carriage this afternoon."

She laughed. "I thought that was a better place than under one of the trees as the youngest children did."

Putting her hand on Bianca's arm, she said, "I am very sorry that I upset you and Aunt Millicent."

"I believe she feared you had been spirited away by the gypsies who have been telling fortunes in their wagon."

"Being a gypsy and ambling from village to village might not be such a bad fate." She raised her hands over her head. "Do you think I could learn their dances?"

"What has gotten into you?" Bianca asked with a laugh. "You do not usually talk like this."

"'Tis festival day. Everyone is someone else on festival day."

A deep voice asked, "Is that so?"

Turning, Bianca smiled at Lucian. He had left his coat and cravat in the carriage, because his London clothes appeared out of place among the villagers' informal dress. She was tempted to tell him that he was drawing even more attention now because he looked much more handsome like this. She must not let Rosie's effervescent festival spirits infect her.

She waited for Rosie to answer. Even a clandestine jab with her elbow brought no response from her sister, who was looking at the ground. Knowing one of them must say something, Bianca said, "It is fun to imagine what one might be."

"An interesting thought." He leaned back against a tree and folded his arms in front of himself. He propped one shiny boot heel against the tree as he smiled at them.

"Whose life would you choose other than your own?" she asked, smiling at Rosie, whose eyes were still downcast. Elbowing her sister again, she was pleased that Rosie stopped staring at the grass. Now she seemed fascinated by a button in the middle of Lucian's shirt.

Lucian grinned at her, then at Rosie. "I suppose I should say that I would be a courageous knight ready to battle any dragon in exchange for no more than a smile from one of the lovely Dunsworthy ladies."

"Uh-huh."

Laughing at the doubt in Bianca's voice, he said, "If you wish the truth, I suppose I would choose a life exploring the ancient wonders of Egypt with my friend Fortenbury." He smiled. "Lord Fortenbury is the brother of Jordan, my friend who is having the gathering to celebrate his final hours of being a bachelor."

"Really?" Rosie asked, a tinge of excitement filling her voice as she raised her head to look at his face. "I have read of those discoveries that were made by the French and then the English during the battles there. They are fascinating."

"I had no idea that you were interested in such things." Lucian's smile broadened, but he could not hide his astonishment that she had spoken to him, unbidden. "We must continue this discussion on our way to Plymouth, Rosie."

Bianca bit her lip to keep from releasing her delight. She had not guessed such a small thing could build a connection between her sister and Lucian. Her apprehension that the match was doomed because of Rosie's bashful ways now could be set aside.

"What would you be, Bianca?" continued Lucian. "Your sister wants to be a gypsy, and I wish to dig in the sands of Egypt."

She started to reply, then realized she did not have an answer. "I don't know."

"Oh, come now," Lucian said with another chuckle. "I have seen that you are a woman with much imagination and determination. You cannot expect me to believe you have no wish to sample a taste of a life other than your own." Turning to Rosie, he asked, "Do you have an idea of what Bianca might wish to be?"

"Excuse me." Rosie ducked away into the crowd.

Bianca sighed, her optimism fading once more. How would a match be possible if Rosie was constantly so bashful with Lucian?

"She does not hide how she feels, does she?" Lucian scowled, then shook his head with a wry smile. "I would take it as a personal insult, save that I have seen she acts the same with everyone other than you or your aunt."

"She was surprisingly forthcoming about her interest in Egyptian things."

He pushed himself away from the tree. Drawing her hand within his arm, he led her through the crowd. "True, but how can we have a discussion on that topic if she will not continue to speak more than a few words to me?"

"I will ask her, for I know she is greatly interested in Egyptian hieroglyphics."

"Then she should speak with Fortenbury. He is quite fascinated with such things. I must own to being more interested in the great structures said to be along the Nile than all the carvings on them." He glanced over his shoulder. "I cannot envision your sister as a gypsy dancer."

"Do not let her quiet ways bamboozle you. Rosie is a very good dancer."

"Is that so?"

"If you do not believe me, ask her to stand up with you and decide for yourself."

"Will she speak to me if I do?"

Bianca frowned. What an outrageous man! "It is your misfortune, my lord, that you live in the present year instead of in medieval times when you could have commanded her to answer."

"Mayhap I should appreciate her bashful silence."

"I know *I* do."

He tugged on the ribbons of her bonnet, but not hard enough to untie them, and chuckled. "I take that as a hint that you are tired of listening to my prattle and wish me to ask Rosie to dance." He bowed deeply from the waist. "I am at your command, my lady."

"Don't call me that," she said, all her amusement and vexation vanishing.

He sobered. "Don't call you what?"

"Don't call me . . . that." She looked around them and hoped no one was eavesdropping. "Lord Dunsworthy is very sensitive to the fact that many of the people in the shire were not pleased to see him assume the title after Kevin's death."

Lucian's eyes widened. "It was not his choice. He was next in line for your brother's title."

"I know that, and you know that, and these people know that in their minds." She sighed as she touched the center of her chest. "But in their hearts, they refuse to accept it."

"Mayhap because they would have preferred a *Lady* Dunsworthy?"

"Lucian, please, say no more about this. Such farradiddles have a way of becoming gossip that could hurt my cousin and the rest of my family." She blinked back the tears she hated. "It is difficult enough for Lord Dunsworthy now. I have no desire to make it more so."

"Is having that title what you aspire to when you think of what you would rather be other than yourself?"

"No, the reason I could not give you an answer is because I am happy being myself." She paused when she heard the musicians playing the notes announcing another country dance was about to begin. "You should ask Rosie now if you wish to dance."

"I will."

Bianca thought he would add something else, but he did not as he walked to where Rosie was standing beside Aunt Millicent. She watched as he bowed and then held out his hand to Rosie. A twinge surprised her when her sister put her fingers on his. This was what she had been working for, so she should be exulting instead of thinking how Lucian's rough hand was always so gentle when it touched hers.

Ignoring that twinge, so she would not have to examine it too closely, she went to stand beside her aunt. Aunt Millicent's eyes were focused on Rosie, who was facing Lucian as the dance began.

Bianca saw her sister smile as Lucian said something as they passed through the pattern of the dance. If Rosie replied, she could not tell because her sister turned away to twirl on Lucian's arm.

Aunt Millicent held out a bowl to Bianca. "Would you like some of these berries and cream? They are delicious."

Taking a bite of the strawberries, Bianca smiled. "You are right. They are delicious."

"I assume that"—she pointed toward the dancers— "I assume that is your doing."

"Rosie and Lucian have discovered they have in common an interest in ancient Egypt, so I thought a dance would offer them a chance to find out what else they might share."

"You are a kindhearted sister to care so much about Rosie."

Bianca took another bite of the berries. "Rosie has long dreamed of a handsome Prince Charming who would come on his charger and sweep her off her feet and into his arms."

"That is true, but what about you? Don't you have dreams of a dashing hero who will win your heart?"

"Mayhap later."

"Later? After what?"

"After I help Rosie make her dream come true. Who knows? It may happen during our journey to Plymouth," she said brightly.

Too brightly, she realized when Aunt Millicent's eyes slitted. "Is that why you asked Lucian to take us with him to Plymouth?"

"He wanted to do something kind to repay us for our care, and taking us on such a sojourn seemed something small that would not leave him feeling obligated to us. His large carriage will easily carry the four of us."

"If making a match between him and your sister is your intention, Bianca, riding in such close quarters might bring about just the opposite result."

"Mayhap Rosie will become accustomed enough to him that she will speak more readily in his company."

"Is that your only reason for this sudden interest in going to Plymouth?"

Bianca smiled to hide her thoughts. Her aunt would be horrified to discover the true reason Bianca wanted to go to Plymouth. Aunt Millicent yearned to put the war out of her mind. So did Bianca, as soon as she fulfilled the pledge she had made in honor of Kevin's memory. If she could speak to Napoleon and release the pain in her heart, she would be able to stop thinking of the past and look to the future.

She patted her aunt's arm. "Playing matchmaker is more fun than I had expected. Why not enjoy it a bit longer?"

"As long as you are certain you are well aware of what you are doing."

"The earl would be a good match for—"

"You."

Her smile faded. "Do not be absurd, Aunt Millicent. Lucian holds Rosie in the highest regard. He treats me like a servant, always trying to order me about and tell me what I should or should not do. It is annoying."

"Annoyance is sometimes the way a man inveigles his way into a woman's heart."

"Do not be absurd," she said again, trying to pay no mind to how her pulse pounded through her at her aunt's comments. Each one brought forth a memory she did not want to think of now, but it was impossible to pay no attention to how her fingers trembled as she recalled his hand holding them. "If I decide to wed, it will be to a man who treats me with respect and kindness."

"Lucian does treat you with both respect and kindness."

"But he also constantly sticks his nose into everything I try to do."

"Because he is interested in you."

"No, it is because he is nosy and interfering and thinks he can do everything better than I can."

Aunt Millicent smiled and turned to look back at the dancers.

Bianca did as well and saw her sister was laughing again, this time with more enthusiasm and a comment, as she took Lucian's hand. Looking down at the bowl Aunt Millicent had given her, she walked back into the crowd to the blanket where she had been sitting that afternoon. She sat and took another spoonful of the berries.

Everything was going just as it should, so she should be happy. Yet she was not. Thoughts of Kevin must have brought her a new case of the dismals. She needed to stop thinking of her brother and concentrate now on her sister. What could she do next to bring Lucian and Rosie together? The journey to Plymouth would take nearly two days in his closed carriage, so she was certain to discover a way to find out what other interests they shared. She smiled. Who would have guessed that her resolve to confront Napoleon would offer this opportunity for her sister?

"If you sit by yourself and grin like a fool, people will begin to wonder about you." Lucian squatted beside her and held out his hand. "Now it is your turn to take a turn to the music."

"No, thank you." She looked past him, but could not see where her sister was. "Rosie—"

"I danced with Rosie, and she was cordial company."

"I am glad. I thought you would be pleasantly surprised once you gave her a chance to get over her shyness."

"So be good company, too, Bianca, and stand up

with me." He put his hand directly in front of her. "You are hesitating. You did not consider me unsuitable to dance with your sister."

"That is true."

"Then I should not be considered unsuitable company for you."

"That is also true."

"So dance with me."

She thought of the many excuses that she could give him. While walking about with Rosie, she had promised Mrs. Emerson to spend some time talking with the dowager about her garden. The vicar had asked her to speak with him about the poor box. Mr. Raymond had mentioned that he wished to discuss the concerns of the villagers about the high speed of the Royal Mail when it drove past the green.

When Lucian offered his hand a third time, all her flimsy excuses vanished. She wanted to dance with him. She wanted a moment of pure fun when she did not have to think about her obligations to her family or anything but the music and dancing. She set the bowl beside her and watched her own fingers settle on his palm before his broad ones closed over them.

As he lifted her hand to his lips, she feared his fever had become contagious. She was suffused with a dazzling pleasure that seemed to be burning outward from her very center. Her gaze was caught by his, and she knew it was more than just wanting to dance. She wanted to dance with *him*. Rosie might be the perfect bride for him, but Bianca could not dampen her reaction to his bold touch.

She let him bring her to her feet and lead her to where the musicians were preparing for the next set. As Lucian drew her out of the crowd toward the open area reserved for dancing, the musicians began to play.

Her steps faltered. "That is a waltz! We do not waltz in Dunstanbury."

"You must know how. When it was expected that you would go to London for a Season, your aunt would have had you tutored in everything you might need to know."

"Yes, I know how to waltz."

"Prove it."

"What?"

He laughed. "Prove that you know how to waltz." He took her hand and placed his other one on her waist.

She had barely time to lift her skirt high enough so she would not trip before he swirled her through the pattern of the dance. Her trepidation that she might have forgotten the steps in the two years since she had last danced it vanished as she matched his steps with an ease that astounded her. He moved with the same grace he had put into every motion since he recovered from his fever.

When she glanced up at him with a smile, she found him watching her with a peculiar intensity. She tried to look away, but was not quick enough. Her gaze was captured again by his. As his fingers splayed across her waist, she was aware of every inch of him close to her. Her heart beat so fiercely she could no longer hear the music. Yet it swirled around them, guiding their steps as if their feet belonged to a single mind.

When he grimaced, she blinked, freed from his gaze. "Is something wrong?" she asked. "Did I step on your toes?"

"No, it is nothing more than this arm which pangs too often and occasionally taunts me with something that is decidedly more than a pang."

"Mayhap we should not finish the dance."

"Are you using my pain as an excuse to put an end to our dance?" He smiled and twirled her around rapidly.

"You are the most vexing man I have ever met."

"Obviously you have not met many men." He chuckled. "There are others far more vexing than I."

She arched her brows as he did. "Allow me to make that decision for myself. I hope you will refrain from irritating me beyond all good sense until we reach Plymouth."

"You are single-minded."

"You are not the only one to describe me that way."

"I would wager your aunt has told you that more than once."

"That is a wager you would win." She copied his superior smile.

"Good, because I like to bet only on things I am certain to win."

"Then it is not a wager."

"That brings to mind another wager that you have resisted discussing."

She smiled. "That I would make a fool of myself in the presence of your friends from among the *ton*?"

"So will you accept my invitation to attend Jordan's gathering in Plymouth?"

"I should speak first to Rosie and Aunt Millicent."

He drew her closer as he lowered his voice. "Why? Rosie and your aunt will enjoy the gathering, I am sure."

She did not reply, instead letting the sweet music

surround her. How Lucian would crow if she owned that he was right! This was pleasant. Most pleasant. Dancing with her brother during lessons with a caper-merchant was nothing like this.

Regret filled her when the melody faded off with its last note. She started to thank Lucian; then she realized no one stood near them. In astonishment, she slowly turned and saw that they had been the only ones dancing. Everyone else had been watching as if they were performing as brazenly as a gypsy dancer would.

"Oh, my!" she gasped.

Lucian offered his arm. Aware of every eye on her, she let him draw her hand within his arm. She was grateful when the musicians began to play another quadrille. Both Rosie and Aunt Millicent were joining this dance.

Aunt Millicent fired a frown in her direction, and Bianca was glad Rosie was tugging their aunt toward the other dancers. Her sister must hope that the time needed for the dance would ease her aunt's anger that Bianca had been so outrageous. Explaining that she had not known what Lucian had planned was a futile defense. She could have walked away from the dance as soon as she realized it was a waltz. She almost laughed at that thought, for she could not imagine having ended the dance a second earlier than she had to.

Instead of pausing among those watching the dancers, Lucian continued walking across the green. His hand over hers on his arm kept her by his side. Too near to his side, for his boot brushed her skirt with each step. As they left the rest of the festival-goers on the opposite side of the green, every step warned her how alone they were in the deepening shadows beyond the lanterns in the trees closer to the dancing.

"Where are we going?" she asked.

"I heard from nearly a dozen villagers that there is something of interest in this direction."

"The carving on the side of the church?"

He glanced at her, and in the moonlight as they stepped out from under the trees, she could see his amazement. "An excellent guess."

"An easy one, because any visitor is quickly told about the carving on the church."

"Would you show it to me?"

Bianca looked up at the moon splashing faint light across the grass. "I don't think you will be able to see it at this hour."

"I would like to try."

"Why don't I show it to you during the daylight?"

"You will not have time to show it to me before we leave for Plymouth."

"When you bring us back—"

He smiled at her. "I thought part of what I agreed to was that I did not have to return with you to Dunstanbury, that I only needed to make certain you were delivered back here."

"You are not coming back here?" If she had only the time while they were in Plymouth to arrange a match between him and her sister, her task was that much greater.

"I did not say that. I said only that it was not part of our agreement." He gestured toward the stone church. "Come and show me the carving I have heard about." He laughed. "Unless, of course, you do not trust yourself."

"Trust myself?"

"To be alone with me."

She yanked her hand off his arm. "You are the most insufferable cur in the world! Good evening."

He caught her arm before she could take more than a step. "Bianca, give me another reason for your hesitation then."

"Another reason? I barely know you. Being alone with you would put a blemish on my reputation."

"And you care so much about that?"

She raised her head and met his eyes squarely. "I would never do anything to bring any shame to my family. You should realize that by now."

"I do realize that." His voice remained serene. "Do you think I would do anything to put a blemish on your reputation, as you put it, or bring shame to your sister and aunt?"

Dampening her lips, which seemed too dry to let her speak, she whispered, "I barely know you, Lucian."

"So you have already said, but I think you know me well enough to know that I want an answer to my question."

"You would never intentionally do anything to bring shame to my family."

His hand slid down her arm to take her fingers again. Putting them on his sleeve, he drew her toward the church.

Bianca gnawed on her lower lip. She should tell him again that going to look at the carving when it was dark was a want-witted thing to do. She did not want to have him ask more questions that she wanted to avoid answering. With his customary insight, he had asked the most pointed question first.

Did she trust herself with him? She must if she was to succeed in having him offer marriage to Rosie. The thoughts that burst through her mind when he touched her should be banished. Everything pointed toward this being a good match, for he had drawn Rosie out of her shyness far more quickly than most people had been able to. She had to think only of that match and forget about her reaction to his gentle, enticing touch.

The Dunstanbury stone church was set back from the green. Its Norman tower had been built at the same time the walls of Dunsworthy Hall had been raised. The wooden door bore scorch marks from a skirmish during the Civil War, but the stained glass installed at the same time as the tower had been unharmed.

Music and the voices from the green grew softer as she went with Lucian to the far side of the building. She heard only the sound of insects and the rustle of some small creature in the high grass next to the foundation.

"What you are looking for is right there beneath the carvings of the saints," she said. "Do you see it?"

"I can see that there are the letters but I have to own that you are right. I cannot read them in the moonlight."

She bent to run her fingers along the worn letters, which were about three inches high. "They say:

Once, twice, thrice—Be it by heaven or by the devil's own device; What joy or grief for one shall be worthy; Shall come the same for each Dunsworthy."

We'd Like to Invite You to Subscribe to Zebra's Regency Romance Book Club and Send You 4 Free Books as Your Introduction! (Worth $19.96!)

If you're a Regency lover, imagine the joy of getting 4 FREE Zebra Regency Romances and then the chance to have these lovely stories delivered to your home each month at the lowest price available! Well, that's our offer to you and here's how you benefit by becoming a Regency Romance subscriber:

- *4 FREE Introductory Regency Romances are delivered to your doorstep (you only pay for shipping & handling)*
- *4 BRAND NEW Regencies are then delivered each month (usually before they're available in bookstores)*
- *Subscribers save almost $4.00 off the cover price every month*
- *You also receive a FREE monthly newsletter, which features author profiles, discounts, subscriber benefits, book previews and more*
- *There's no risks or obligations...in other words, you can cancel whenever you wish with no questions asked*

Join the thousands of readers who enjoy the savings and convenience offered to Regency Romance subscribers. After your initial introductory shipment, you'll receive 4 brand-new Zebra Regency Romances each month to examine for 10 days. Then, if you decide to keep the books, you pay the preferred subscriber's price, plus shipping and handling.

It's a no-lose proposition, so return the FREE BOOK CERTIFICATE today!

A $19.96 value – **FREE** No obligation to buy anything – ever.
4 FREE BOOKS are waiting for you! Just mail in the certificate below!

FREE BOOK CERTIFICATE

YES! Please rush me 4 FREE Zebra Regency Romances (I only pay $1.99 for shipping and handling).I understand that each month thereafter I will be able to preview 4 brand-new Regency Romances FREE for 10 days. Then, if I should decide to keep them, I will pay the money-saving preferred subscriber's price for all 4... (that's a savings of 20% off the retail price), plus shipping and handling. I may return any shipment within 10 days and owe nothing and I may cancel this subscription at any time.

Name_____

Address_____ Apt._____

City_____ State_____ Zip_____

Telephone (_____)_____

Signature_____

(If under 18, parent or guardian must sign)

Offer limited to one per household and not to current subscribers. Terms, offer and prices subject to change. Orders subject to acceptance by Regency Romance Book Club. Offer Valid in the U.S. only.

RN104A

Say Yes to 4 Free Books!

Complete and return the order card to receive your FREE books, a $19.96 value!

If the certificate is missing below, write to:

Regency Romance Book Club,

P.O. Box 5214,

Clifton, NJ 07015-5214

or call TOLL-FREE
1-800-770-1963

Visit our website at
www.kensingtonbooks.com

Treat yourself to 4 FREE Regency Romances!
A $19.96 VALUE... FREE!
No obligation to buy anything ever!

lll..l..lll....lll.l.l.l...l..lll.l.l.l...lll.ll.l...ll...l

REGENCY ROMANCE BOOK CLUB

Zebra Home Subscription Service, Inc.

P.O. Box 5214

Clifton NJ 07015-5214

Standing, she laughed. "It is something learned by every Dunsworthy child as soon as he or she can read."

"No wonder you are so close to your sister and aunt. You do not want them to cause any trouble that will be exacted upon you as well." He chuckled. "I would believe it is more likely to be the other way around. They keep a close eye on you."

"I doubt this old rhyme that was put here when the church was built in the twelfth century has any influence over anything we do now." She smiled. "But I have always liked the fact that it is here—it connects us to our past." She turned to walk back to the green.

His hand on her arm halted her as it had on the green. "Not that way. You should not walk counterclockwise around the church."

"Mayhap I wish to walk widdershins so I can call forth the fairy folk."

"Or the devil." Lucian chuckled. "Now there is a chap who would not flinch at a wager."

Bianca shook her head with a smile. "I am not the only one who could be accused of being single-minded."

"No, you are the one using every possible excuse not to give me an answer." He pointed at the letters carved into the stone. "That says you can make the decision, and it will be accepted by your family."

"You are being ludicrous." She pulled her arm out of his grasp. "My family does not make its decisions based on an old superstition."

"So make a decision, Bianca. Will you accept my invitation to Jordan's assembly?"

She almost shook her head again, then paused. In the elegance of the gathering at the home of Lucian's friend, where everyone was anticipating a wedding, surely the aura of romance would persuade both Lucian and Rosie to think of a match of their own.

"Yes," she replied.

Even in the dim light, she could see his eyes grow wide with incredulity. "Amazing, Bianca. You argue and argue, and then you agree with such alacrity." He smiled. "You need not worry about not knowing the other guests. I will happily alert you to which ones could be troublesome for you and your family."

"Please do not patronize me. I have been in the company of the Polite World."

"When you were little more than a child."

"I attended a wedding of my father's goddaughter shortly before Kevin bought his commission."

He looked out into the darkness. "A most foolish thing for him to do."

"He could not be talked out of it."

"I understand."

"He was determined to serve England and halt the threat of Napoleon's dreams of an empire."

"That I understand as well." His voice was hushed.

"I wish I could understand," she said, picking a long-stemmed piece of grass. "He thought it would be this great escapade like the stories we used to tell each other."

He grasped her shoulders and turned her to face him. "His misconception is a common one. Very common." His mouth twisted in a wry smile. "I shared it myself."

"But you returned alive."

"I know how fortunate I was then . . . and now." He drew her a half step toward him.

Unsure what he planned, but fearing he might do something that would ruin her hopes for a match between him and Rosie, she tried to edge away. He did not release her. Wanting to see his shadowed face so she would be able to guess his intentions, she said, "Rosie will enjoy attending your friend's fête."

"I am sure." He brushed her hair back with a single fingertip.

The touch of his skin against her cheek shattered her already fragile composure, for the caress sent shivers through her. She fought to extinguish them as she said, "Rosie may be shy, but she will be delighted to have this opportunity to glimpse the Polite World."

"I am sure." He twisted the strand around his finger and ran it along her cheek, then along his.

Her breath caught, and she could not speak as she stared into the glistening pools of his eyes. Even the darkness was unable to hide the strong emotions in them.

"Rosie will like to see the fancy gowns of the guests," she murmured. She closed her eyes as his finger dropped the strand of hair and stroked the curve of her jaw, lingering on the surprisingly sensitive skin behind her ear.

"And do you think Rosie would like this?"

He folded her hands between his before lifting them one at a time to his mouth. His kisses sent renewed quivers through her. Bringing her closer, he bent toward her, and she held her breath. She should push him aside, for his intentions could not be honorable. He was an earl, and she was the poor daughter of a profligate baron. Her reputation was all she had left. She must not let him tarnish it.

But he said he would do nothing to shame my family, argued the part of her mind urging her to touch him as he was touching her.

Confusion became a different emotion, softer, but infinitely stronger, while she raised her gaze along his chin to the firm line of his lips. Seeing them tilt in a beguiling smile, a warmth dripped through her that had nothing to do with the fragrant breeze drifting from the green. Only with effort did she pull her gaze away from his lips to lift it to his shadowed eyes.

His hands framed her face as he whispered her name as no one else had ever spoken it. Gently, desperately, clutching onto each syllable as if it were a lifeline. Then he was kissing her, and her senses careened out of control. She had never imagined the fire that would burn upon his lips and surge through her. His arms slipped around her, and he brought her up against his strong chest. His fingers sliding along her back pressed her even closer as he deepened the kiss until her lips softened beneath his tender assault. She curved her arms around his shoulders, taking care not to brush his left arm. She was curling her hand around his nape when he abruptly released her.

She stared up at him. When he chuckled, she recoiled as if he had struck her. Her horror grew when he asked, "So do you think Rosie will like that?"

She could not speak. Was this his way of repaying her for insisting that he dance with Rosie? He had enjoyed that, hadn't he? She shuddered, knowing she had enjoyed his kiss, too.

He laughed again, and her hand struck his cheek before she could halt it. She rushed back toward the green. He had been dallying with both her and her sister. Had she made a terrible mistake in plotting a match between him and Rosie? She hoped she would not find out in Plymouth that the answer was yes.

Chapter Eight

The carriage was waiting in front of the cottage. Moss was giving the harness on the left-hand horse a final check. Sitting in the carriage, Lucian read the newspaper that Moss had delivered to him with a long face this morning. The gossip about the duel in the middle of St. James's had the *ton* abuzz with speculation about Andover's claims of Lucian calling on his mistress. Lucian knew that there would be many questions at Jordan's gathering, but that did not bother him. He would gladly explain what a beefhead Andover was. If his protests went unheard, he had Bullock as a witness to the contretemps as well as the many other people Andover had insulted.

He heard the coachee call, "The bags are stored in the boot, Miss Dunsworthy." Moss's voice was cheerful, for he could not hide his relief that they were continuing the journey that had been interrupted for a fortnight.

Which Miss Dunsworthy was Moss talking to? Lucian looked out and smiled. Bianca. He folded the newspaper and put it in the small bag by his feet.

This trip was going to be more interesting than he had guessed when he went with the Dunsworthys to the village festival two days ago. He had not expected

Bianca to flee like a frightened child when he had kissed her by the church. That she had slapped his cheek first was not, he had to own, a surprise. He had deserved the facer for being so bold, but he had not been able to resist the chance to show her that matchmaking could be a very perilous undertaking for the matchmaker.

He reached to open the door, but paused. How sweet and innocent her lips had been beneath his. He had almost forgotten himself and his intention to tease her in the enchantment of that single kiss. She had fit so well in his arms. If he had not released her and laughed to break the spell of holding her close, he did not know where that kiss might have led. The consideration of those possibilities had kept him from sleeping well the past two nights. His mind was filled with images of her astonishment as he tipped her mouth beneath his. Her lips had tasted of berries, and her hair was scented with sunshine.

Other voices spilled from the house, and knowing he could not lurk in the carriage, he opened its door. Stepping out, he smiled at Bianca. She gave him a cool nod as she held her reticule in front of her. He was tempted to tell her it made a flimsy shield. She shifted it to her left hand as if she realized the same thing.

"I am well," he said when she was silent.

"I did not ask how you were doing." She glanced at him and then away again quickly.

"But you have every other day upon our first encounter, so I thought I would be thoughtful and save you the trouble of having to ask."

"You are very kind."

He wanted to chuckle at her sarcasm, but that

would infuriate her more. "Would you like a hand in?"

"As soon as Aunt Millicent and Rosie get here."

"Afraid to be in the carriage with only me?" asked Lucian.

"Do not be silly. Even you must be gentleman enough to recall your manners in the light of day." She clasped both hands over her reticule again.

Hearing what sounded suspiciously like muffled laughter from the other side of the carriage, Lucian knew Moss was listening closely. What else had the coachee chanced to hear? Bianca's sister and aunt continued to treat Lucian with the same kindness they had since before the festival, so he doubted Bianca had told them that he had kissed her. Yet, somehow, Moss seemed to have gotten wind of it.

Mayhap he was being silly. Moss had been at the carriage, not skulking through the shadows around the church. Lucian could not allow his own unsettled thoughts to lead him to accuse someone else of misdeeds.

A good night's sleep, that was what he needed. A deep rest and dreams that were not invaded by blue-gray eyes gazing up at him.

"I try never to forget my manners," Lucian replied, knowing he would be a fool to reveal even a hint of his thoughts. She would either slap his face again or laugh; either alternative was ignoble.

Bianca's tone was crisp. "Then you must endeavor not to forget yourself."

Her words mirrored his own thoughts so closely he was not sure how to answer. As he admired how her yellow gown seemed to bring out every glimmer of gold in her hair, which was primly pulled back beneath her bonnet, he could not keep from imagining it flowing free and soft over his hands.

"You know Widow Morehouse's younger son will take good care of Barley and the cats while we are gone," Millicent was saying as she closed the cottage door. "Stop fretting over them, Rosie." She smiled as she came down the short path between the trees. "Good morning, Lucian. I have to say we chose a lovely day to begin our journey."

The weather. That was a safe topic, and he was glad when Millicent began to talk about storms that had ravaged this shore before the one that had sent him to their cottage. Rosie added a few more details on another storm during the winter, astonishing him. Mayhap she had begun to blossom in his company at the very moment her sister had decided to shut him out. It was going to be a long, uncomfortable journey.

Bianca listened to the excitement in Rosie's voice and the happiness in Aunt Millicent's as Moss gave a final check of the carriage. She wished she could share that anticipation of the journey to Plymouth and the gathering at Mr. Jordan's house. How could she when she was unsure what Lucian might do next? She had not guessed he would kiss her by the church, but she knew he must not kiss her again. His attentions should be for Rosie.

Yet she could not stop thinking of how splendid his arms around her had been. She must find a way to push those thoughts from her head and concentrate on proving to Lucian that Rosie would make him the perfect bride. She wished she knew how. Had he or anyone else noticed how often she stared at his lips?

She would look away, but her gaze was pulled again and again to them as her own tingled with the memory of his mouth over hers.

She stepped back as Moss came around the carriage to put the last of the bags into the boot. Giving him a stiff smile, she edged past Aunt Millicent and Rosie, who were both talking with Lucian. She climbed into the carriage without assistance and sat on the seat facing forward. She settled her reticule on her lap. It bulged with the last few things she had forgotten to pack. Surely Lucian would be a gentlemen today and take the backward seat, so she would not have to sit beside him. But would looking at him all day leave her more bewildered?

"I did not see you get in," Aunt Millicent said as she stepped into the carriage with Lucian's help. Sitting beside Bianca, she smoothed her dress. "You have been uncommonly quiet this morning."

"I have nothing to say."

"You? You always have something to say about everything, Bianca." Her aunt laughed and moved her knees to the side so Rosie could come into the carriage. Setting a small bag by the door, Rosie sat across from Bianca.

"Not today."

She saw her aunt's eyes narrow when Lucian entered the now-crowded carriage. Mayhap Aunt Millicent understood what Bianca could not say. Lucian had taken advantage of the good will of the festival to kiss her without so much as her say-so. Then he had laughed at her. Laughed! As if the wondrous sensations had been nothing but a joke to him. Mayhap they had been, but she had been overmastered by her very first kiss.

As the carriage began to move, Rosie could not hide her delight with the whole of the journey and the gathering in Plymouth. Rosie's smile added to her delicate beauty, which was guaranteed to draw the gentlemen's eyes at Mr. Jordan's house. Aunt Millicent would keep a close watch on her younger niece, and Bianca would as well. Not that Bianca worried about her sister coming to grief in a man's arms—as she had! She forced that thought aside and concentrated instead on Aunt Millicent's long list of things not to do when in the presence of the Polite World. Bianca was certain that Rosie would take each admonition to heart. She must, too.

Last night, Rosie had come into the bedroom she had shared with Bianca while Lucian was recuperating. Sitting on the bed, where Bianca was reading a book, she said, "Bianca, I am fearful of what will happen when we reach Plymouth."

"Do not fret. From what Aunt Millicent has told us about the Polite World, you can ask a single question and that will propel conversation for the next hour."

"But what question?"

"We shall work on that after we meet Lucian's friends. That first evening, we shall be so busy being introduced to the other guests that I doubt we shall be required to make much conversation."

Rosie had been comforted, at least a bit. Her bright eyes this morning displayed her anticipation with the country house gathering. Bianca had to own that she also looked forward to it, because she had longed for a glimpse into the closed world of the *ton*. All they had to do was endure this carriage ride for almost two days.

"Henry Jordan is easily bored," Lucian was saying in response to a question her aunt must have asked. "That he has decided to wed was a surprise for all, because nobody had thought he would tie himself down when it is his brother's obligation to produce an heir to the family's title."

"He must really love this young woman," Aunt Millicent said with a smile.

"I understand that love does cause a person to do very peculiar things."

Her aunt chuckled. "That sounds as if you have never been afflicted with this particular malady, Lucian."

"I must own I have had a mild case or two, but each time the condition passed swiftly. My time with the *ton* has been somewhat limited, first by my father's death and then by other obligations."

Bianca looked at him for the first time since they had settled themselves in the carriage. Startled when she realized he was staring at her, she could not look away. Fatigue weighed his face. Had he not slept because he was making preparations for their journey, or had other thoughts kept him awake? She was tempted to ask him if he suffered from guilt that he had taken advantage of the festival and the moonlight to kiss her. It was impossible to speak of that when her aunt and sister would hear.

What could she say to turn his attention away from her and back toward Rosie? Now that they were on their way to where Napoleon was being held in Plymouth Harbor, she should think only of her resolve to speak her mind to the former emperor. She owed that much to Kevin.

Rosie did not give her a chance to reply, for her sister said with fervor, "I hope I am never too busy when love comes my way. I would hate to have it pass me by."

"I am sure it will be patient and wait for you to take notice of it," Bianca said, patting her sister's hand.

"And you?" Rosie asked.

"Do you mean that I will be watching for love to come to you? Of course." She laughed, although it sounded forced, for she wished Rosie had not embarked on this subject when Lucian was listening with a half smile. "Who knows? It may come calling on you this very weekend."

"I doubt anyone will notice me in my outmoded clothes."

Lucian's smile widened. "And *I* doubt anyone will take note of what you are wearing when the three lovely Dunsworthy ladies come into the room."

"It is an informal gathering, and Bianca has redone several dresses for you," added Aunt Millicent when Rosie huddled back against the cushions, obviously unsure how to respond after her excitement had compelled her to speak up in Lucian's company. "You will be fine, Rosie. It is not as if you are going to Almack's."

"Thank heavens," Lucian said.

"You do not like Almack's?" asked Bianca before she could halt herself. Like Rosie, she was allowing the excitement of the trip to Plymouth to unleash comments she should keep to herself.

Lucian draped an arm along the back of the seat, taking care not to touch Rosie. With a cynical smile, he said, "It is not a place to enjoy, Bianca. It is a place to endure. If one passes the standards of the patronesses, one still must meet the expectations of everyone else in Almack's."

"Was that a problem for you?" she asked, her voice as cool as his.

"Bianca!" chided her aunt, and Lucian's eyes crinkled with his grin. "I trust you did not leave your manners at the cottage." Looking at Lucian, Aunt Millicent added, "You describe one aspect of Almack's quite well."

"Have you been there?" he asked.

"Once, as a very nervous young miss. I saw what you describe, but I was fascinated by the glorious clothes and the quick-witted conversation."

Lucian reached into the bag by his feet. Papers crackled. Pulling out a newspaper, he offered it to Aunt Millicent. "Moss found this somewhere. I do not delve too deeply into his methods when he is successful. Mayhap you would like to read it. There might be a mention of some of the people you will be meeting at Jordan's."

"Imagine that!" Aunt Millicent exclaimed, sounding as thrilled as Rosie. "We may be meeting people written about in the newspaper."

"As long as it is not about some criminals who have been nabbed," Bianca said.

Lucian chuckled. "I always try to choose law-abiding companions."

"Like the man who shot you in St. James's?" Bianca asked as Aunt Millicent opened the newspaper and handed several pages to Rosie.

"He is not anyone I would choose as a companion, even before he was so want-witted." He scowled as his eyes drilled her.

She did not lower her eyes, even when her aunt

scolded her again, this time for speaking of the incident. Instead she looked at the back of the pages Rosie was reading. One page was filled with a series of articles about Parliament. The other listed figures for the year's estimated harvests. Mayhap the other side of the paper was more interesting, because Rosie seemed engrossed.

When nobody spoke, Bianca realized her aunt had taken another page to read while Lucian was staring out the window as if he wanted to avoid missing an inch of their journey. She considered asking if there were more pages of the newspaper, but leaned back against her seat and looked out her own window.

The pages Aunt Millicent held brushed Bianca's lap as she lowered them. "Lucian, there appears to be a page missing. Is it still in your bag?"

Taking the pages from her, he scanned them and nodded. "You are right. There is a page missing."

"Mayhap it was lost while coming down from London," Aunt Millicent said as she took the pages Rosie had been reading and settled back to enjoy them. "Thank you, Lucian, for sharing these. It is a treat to have the chance to read the *Morning Chronicle*."

"There may be newer editions at Jordan's house." He tapped the date on the front page. "This one is more than a week old."

"Nevertheless, it is a pleasure to read it."

Rosie reached for the pages Aunt Millicent had finished, then put her hand over her stomach. Her face twisted for a moment.

"Are you all right?" Bianca asked.

"You worry too much about me." Rosie gave her a smile, keeping her gaze from moving to the other side of the carriage. She now was willing to talk in Lucian's company, but still seldom spoke directly to him. "I believe I ate breakfast too quickly this morning in anticipation of beginning our sojourn." She lifted the pages to read them.

The back of these pages held no more interest for Bianca than the other ones. The news articles were interspersed with gossip. Again she looked out the window to watch the rhythm of the waves on the shore that the road paralleled. It was comforting in its consistency when so much unknown awaited them in Plymouth.

In spite of Lucian's assumptions that they would be welcome at Mr. Jordan's estate, Bianca was not so sure. She did not care for herself, because she had little interest in rubbing elbows with the *ton,* but both Rosie and Aunt Millicent were thrilled with the invitation.

Some sense that has no name teased her to look toward the other side of the carriage. Knowing she should not give in to it, she was unable to resist its pull. She turned her head, and her eyes locked with Lucian's. With her sister and aunt holding up the pages of the newspaper, it was as if she and Lucian were alone behind a curtain.

His hand covered hers on her lap. She considered pulling her hand away, but then his fingers would be upon her leg. Just imagining the powerful longings that would surge through her at such an intimate touch sent a shiver down her back.

He slowly smiled, and she guessed he had felt the tremor created by her fantasy. How much greater a fool could she be? She opened her reticule and drew out the needle she had brought along for when she had a chance to repair the loose ruffle on Rosie's best dress.

His smile did not waver as she held up the pin. Rather, it broadened as he winked at her. How brazen could one man be? She wanted to dress him down more heatedly than Aunt Millicent had her, but she said nothing. She looked from the pin to him, and he chuckled silently. He did not need to say anything either as his gaze dropped to her hand before rising back to her face. If she jabbed at his hand with the pin, he would snatch his hand away, and she might end up pricking herself. He caressed her fingers, daring her to put her thoughts into action. She raised the pin.

The newspaper page fell onto her lap, and her sister groaned. Reaching for Rosie, she paused when she realized she still held the pin.

"Give it to me," Lucian said, all humor gone from his voice.

Handing him the pin, Bianca put her hands on her sister's arm. "Rosie, what is wrong?"

Her sister's mouth twisted.

"What is it?"

"My stomach." She pressed her hand to her middle. "I fear I shall be ill."

Lucian opened the small door on the roof and called, "Moss, stop the carriage. Now!"

"Yes, my lord," came the answer, along with a command to the horses to slow.

Aunt Millicent said, "Sweet heavens, Rosie. You are nearly as green as the grass."

Bianca leaned her sister's head in her lap and stroked Rosie's hair. Her sister shuddered with attempts not to embarrass herself in front of them.

As the carriage rolled to a stop, Lucian threw open the door. He stepped out and lifted Rosie from the seat. When he started to carry her to a grassy mound by the hedgerow, she shook her head and moaned.

"Bianca!" She put her hand over her mouth as her face became a more odious green.

Jumping out, Bianca ran to them. Poor Rosie was mortified at the idea of being ill in Lucian's presence. If that happened, Rosie would never lower her bashful barrier to him again.

"Set her down, Lucian."

"By the roadside?" he asked.

"Yes."

"She will get dirty if—"

"Set her down! Now!"

He complied without another comment and stepped back.

Bianca knelt in the dust as her sister wretched. Looking over her shoulder, she said, "Lucian, she would like some privacy."

Lucian nodded and walked back to the carriage where Millicent was alighting. He saw her worry and said, "She should be fine, Millicent. Carriage-sickness is troublesome, but never fatal."

She smiled briefly at his attempt to ease her fears. "I should have remembered she was often bothered by carriage-sickness as a child. Riding backwards only made it worse, I am sure."

"She rode backwards to the village and did not complain." He paused and frowned. "But as I recall, she was even quieter than usual, and she was a bit wobbly on her feet when she arrived at the festival. I should have remembered that."

"Do not berate yourself," she replied. "Rosie could have said something."

Lucian looked at the two sisters. Rosie was sitting on her heels, and Bianca was wiping her sister's forehead with a handkerchief. No one could doubt the affection between the Dunsworthy sisters. Had Bianca spoken to her sister about wanting to avoid him? As much as Rosie adored her sister, would she have been willing to risk her stomach by sitting beside him in the carriage? Blast! The situation was growing more and more complicated, and giving Bianca a teasing kiss had just worsened the situation.

"Moss?" he called.

His coachee jumped down from the box. "Yes, my lord?"

"Get a bottle from the boot."

Moss rushed to the back of the carriage and swiftly returned with an open bottle of wine.

Thanking him, Lucian took it and carried it to Bianca. "This might help." He gave her a wry smile. "I am afraid there is no glass, so she will have to drink right from the bottle."

"Where did you get this?"

"I have learned it is a good idea to have a few bottles in the carriage in case there is a need for it."

He saw curiosity in her eyes, and he guessed she wanted to ask him what other circumstances required having wine. Now was not the time to tell her how he had paused at his house in London long enough to collect a few in the hope that the wine might ease the pain in his arm.

For once, she did not ask questions, but held the bottle up to Rosie's lips. "Take a small drink," she murmured.

Rosie shook her head, pressing her hands to her stomach. "I may be sick again if I do."

"A single drink may help settle your stomach."

With obvious reluctance, Rosie agreed. Bianca waited with a patience he had not guessed she had while Rosie swallowed, then held the bottle to Rosie's mouth again. This time, Rosie drank a bit more.

Bianca handed the bottle back to him and helped her sister to her feet. Shoving the bottle into Moss's hands, Lucian put his arm around Rosie to guide her back to the carriage. She might have whispered her thanks, but he could not be certain because she moaned and clutched her stomach again.

Millicent put her hand on Rosie's forehead. "You have no fever, thank heavens. Even so, mayhap it would be for the best if we were to return home."

"No!" cried Bianca. Her high color contrasted so vividly with her sister's ashen cheeks.

"Bianca, do not be selfish." Her aunt scowled at her. "There may be another opportunity to go to a country weekend."

"Do not scold Bianca, Aunt Millicent," Rosie said, leaning against her sister. "I told her already that I want to continue on to Plymouth."

Millicent shook her head. "If you arrive ill, Rosie, you will not be able to enjoy any of the festivities."

"I can switch seats with Bianca, and I should be fine."

If the situation had been different, Lucian would have laughed at the dismay that flew into Bianca's expressive eyes. The idea of sitting beside him was battling with her yearning to make certain her sister would not become ill again.

"I would be glad to ride backward," Bianca said

quietly. She did not add *even if I have to sit beside Lucian,* but he could hear it in her voice.

"Let me help you back into the carriage if you are ready to continue," he said, offering Rosie his hand.

"Thank you." She put her foot on the step. Taking a deep breath, she added in a flurry of words as if she feared she would not get them all out if she hesitated, "I am sorry to disrupt our journey."

His smile became sincere. "You are the least bothersome disruption on this trip."

Lucian saw Bianca's frown, and he chuckled under his breath. No doubt, she saw his words as another failure in her matchmaking attempts. He was tempted to be honest with her and tell her that the only wedding he wished to attend any time soon was Henry Jordan's. But that would mean giving up his chance to feed her a bit of her own medicine this weekend. Not for anything would he miss seeing her face when she discovered how he had discovered her scheme and had created a matchmaking plan of his own.

Guilt taunted him as he sat next to Bianca in the carriage. He admired Bianca's devotion to her family, and he owed her the duty of saving his life. Taking her and her family to Plymouth would not even that debt. As well, he enjoyed her company and her opinions, no matter how illogical he might believe them to be. She clearly thought many of his notions were absurd and was unafraid to let him know that. He appreciated that honesty. If only she were as honest about her silly attempts to get him to offer for her sister. Getting her to own to the truth was a challenge he could not resist.

Especially when it gave him the opportunity to be with Bianca. The light fragrance of whatever she had used to wash her hair filled every breath he took. As the carriage began to roll along the road again, he wondered if he should forget about playing the matchmaker this weekend. Rather than persuade a friend to pay her compliments and betwattle her with attention, he could use the days to show her that a single kiss, stolen in the shadows of a church, was only the beginning of what they could share.

He turned his head to look at her profile, which was so perfectly outlined by the bright sunshine coming into the carriage. His finger begged him to let it trace the silhouette from the tip of her bonnet down her pert nose and over her enticing lips before dropping along the slender line of her neck to the curves hidden beneath her demure gown. This weekend . . .

He smiled. Jordan's house was reputed to have extensive gardens with a few follies hidden among them. A tryst in one of them would be the perfect way to spend a warm afternoon. He had to fight his hands, which wanted to pull her into his arms and show her now a sample of what they could enjoy.

"Must you stare?" she asked in little more than a whisper. He guessed she did not want her aunt and sister to hear. They were both sitting back with their eyes closed. Rosie's face had lost its sickly color, and Millicent's mouth was tilted in a relieved smile.

"Yes."

"What?" she gasped.

He chuckled, knowing that his answer had jolted her. That was all for the good, because everything about this woman endlessly startled him. Her honed wit, her kind heart, her beauty, which while not as classic as her sister's, drew his eyes far more frequently than Rosie's. His chuckle faded as the longing to hold her became an agony. Either he must persuade her to come back into his arms soon, or he must turn some other man's attention to her, so he could put aside this powerful need.

"You are impossible!" she went on.

"Who is to say what is impossible?"

She wore a puzzled expression before she looked out the window again. Her hands lay clasped in her lap, and he noted how her knuckles bleached.

He leaned back against the cushions and closed his eyes. This weekend was sure to be far more challenging—and more interesting—than he had guessed.

Chapter Nine

Bianca opened her eyes as the carriage slowed to a stop. She had never guessed how boring it was to ride for hour after hour in a closed vehicle.

"Awake?" Lucian's whisper came from very close to her ear.

Looking up at him, she was amazed that his hair was as gray as if he had aged several decades. She forgot about the road dust that settled on them when she realized her head was propped against his chest. She started to sit, but his arm around her shoulders kept her from moving away.

"Wake slowly," he murmured.

"I should not—"

His hushed laugh silenced her. "Why not? Your dozing aunt has her head leaning against your sister, who is also quite soundly asleep."

Bianca looked across the dusky interior. Sure enough, Aunt Millicent and Rosie were jumbled together just as Lucian said. But that did not give countenance to Bianca putting her head on his chest. If he thought she had intentionally leaned against him, he might believe she had forgiven him for his outrageous behavior the night of the festival.

She started to raise her head, then stifling a yawn,

put her hand covered with fine grit from the road to her mouth. "Where are we?" It was impossible to halt the yawn, and it escaped.

"At the inn where we will stay tonight." He yawned, too. "Yawning is contagious, I fear."

"It may be that you are tired."

"No, for I had a very pleasant nap with you cuddled close to me."

Bianca pulled back so sharply her bonnet hit the wall of the carriage. Even as her head ached, she kept her voice low. She did not want her sister and aunt to awaken and be privy to this conversation. "Why do you continue to act in such a gauche manner with me?"

"I thought you wished honesty from me, and I can most honestly tell you that it was pleasant to have you nestled here against me."

"A bit less honesty might be appropriate, under the cramped circumstances."

"As you wish." He bowed his head toward her. "Does that prove to you that I am a gentleman?"

She smiled in spite of herself. He was too charming when he was not vexing her beyond all rational thought. "Mayhap it would be for the best that I am not too honest in answering that question."

"Mayhap." His lips quirked, ruining his attempt to appear somber.

"Then I shall say such an action might be the very proof I have been seeking."

He cupped her chin in his hand. "And what else are you seeking, Bianca?"

For the duration of a single heartbeat, she was tempted to divulge the truth. She imagined how he would applaud her pledge to address Napoleon and how he might help her achieve that goal. Then as his finger stroked her cheek and her heart began to pound within her, she let her mind drift in a different direction. What would he say if she told him that what she was seeking was the very thing he had offered to her in his kiss?

Before he laughed at me.

That thought freed her from the spell he had spun about her once more with a single question. She must not let him overmaster her as he had by the church, for she would not offer him another chance to be amused at her expense.

"What am I seeking?" she asked as she lifted her chin out of his hand. "I am seeking a filling supper and a good night's sleep."

"An excellent suggestion." He opened the door and stepped out. "I shall see to it while you wake your aunt and sister."

The carriage bounced when Moss jumped down from the box. Lucian signaled to him, and the two men spoke to each other by the walk leading to the inn's front door. She could not help wondering what Lucian did not wish her to hear.

Aunt Millicent opened one eye. "At last," she breathed with relief. Sitting straighter, she brushed dust from the shawl around her shoulders. "I had forgotten how uncomfortable one can become while riding all day in a carriage with the only stops being for a quick meal and the horses."

"Fortunately, if we kept to the schedule Moss had set, we are more than halfway to Plymouth," Bianca replied as she shook her sister gently to wake her. "He told me at midday that, precluding any bad weather, we should be at Mr. Jordan's house before tea tomorrow."

Rosie sat up and rubbed her eyes. "Thank heavens.

I thought this would be exciting, but it has been a bore." She smiled sleepily. "Save for me getting sick. Thank you, Bianca, for switching seats with me."

"It is such a small thing. Do not mention it."

"It is not a small thing when I know you would have rather continued to sit next to Aunt Millicent," her sister said as they alighted from the carriage. "I have seen how Lucian unnerves you."

"You have?" She wanted to ask how she had betrayed herself to her sister, but had no chance as Aunt Millicent motioned for them to join her on the path to the inn.

The inn must have been built when Elizabeth was queen. The timbered front was darkened with dust from the road, but the walk was edged with flowers, and another pot stood on the pair of steps leading up to the door. Diamond mullions decorated each window on the first floor, but the upper floors had simple windows with single panes. The stableyard was to the right. Another carriage and two wagons were waiting by the unpainted fence. The sound of laughter and chatter came from the stable, which was almost the size of the inn. A horse neighed, and a pair of dogs barked.

While Moss unloaded the carriage with the help of two lads who appeared from around the side of the building, Aunt Millicent inspected Bianca and Rosie as if they were entering Mr. Jordan's fine house instead of a simple roadside inn. Straightening the brim of Rosie's hat, she picked a strand of hair off Bianca's. She held it up and raised her eyebrows.

"Why are you looking at me like that?" Bianca asked.

"This is much shorter than yours, and it is the ebony of Lucian's hair."

As Rosie giggled, Bianca shrugged with what she hoped would appear to be indifference. "If the man sheds upon me, I cannot be faulted for that."

"But this was on the other side of your bonnet from where you were sitting."

Bianca plucked the hair from her aunt's fingers and threw it up into the breeze off the sea. It twirled and vanished. "You are making much ado about the silliest thing. No doubt it fell there when we were helping Rosie."

"No doubt." Aunt Millicent's eyes sparkled as she smiled.

She did not reply, wondering if Aunt Millicent had awakened sometime during the ride to discover Bianca resting her head against Lucian's chest. Even if Aunt Millicent had seen them sitting close, Bianca had not done anything for which she deserved a scold. And she could not be chided for the thoughts she had not acted upon.

She hoped her distress was not visible and was very glad when they entered the dusky inn. Hearing her aunt release her breath once again with a sigh of relief, she knew Aunt Millicent had feared the inn would be beneath her standards of cleanliness.

Indeed, the inn appeared far more well-kept inside than it had from the exterior. Pots of flowers covered every flat surface in the hallway that ran from the front door to the back of the inn where a garden was visible through another open door. From an arch to the right, voices from what Bianca guessed was a taproom flowed out into the foyer. In the other direction, a staircase rose into deeper shadows. Light from windows revealed another room beyond it, but she could not see if it was a common room or the innkeeper's private quarters.

From that direction, a woman bustled toward them, wiping her hands on an apron. It was splattered and stained with ale, so she must have been working in the taproom earlier. She gave a bob toward them as she said, "'is lordship said ye would be 'ere. If ye are willin', follow me. 'is lordship said t'take ye to yer room before sup is served."

"Will you have clean water brought up?" asked Aunt Millicent as they followed the woman up the stairs. They had to duck on the first landing, so they would not hit their heads.

Bianca smiled as she imagined how Lucian would have to crouch to get past that low ceiling. Mayhap he would choose to sleep with Moss in the stable instead. Her smile faded. Thinking about him constantly was witless and chanced allowing herself to get into another predicament that would allow him to laugh at her.

The room where they were taken was high beneath the eaves and stretched from the front of the inn to the back. Windows offered a view of rolling hills on one side and the ocean on the other. This room, too, was a pleasant surprise, for the uneven floorboards had been swept clean. The furniture, although simple, shone with care. A bed that was big enough for two was set by the fieldstone chimney, and a narrower bed flanked it on the other side. A washstand placed by the back window matched a table where two pitchers of water and a bowl waited beneath a scratched glass. Hooks on the wall would hold their clothes while they slept in the beds, whose linen looked as if it had been washed since the last occupants had rented this room.

"Water be 'ere. I can send up one of the girls," the innkeeper said, "if ye'd like some 'elp with gettin' ready for sup."

"That is not necessary." Aunt Millicent smiled tiredly. "We can manage without help."

"Yes, madam." She went to the door. "'is lordship asked fer sup to be ready as soon as I can get it on the table. It should be waitin' by the time ye clean the dirt of the road from ye."

Rosie rushed to the glass and peered into it as the woman went out and closed the door. Touching her face, she grimaced. "We are filthy."

Bianca poured water into the bowl and handed her sister one of the clean cloths stacked under the wash-stand. "A little water will clean that right away."

"Thank heavens no one saw us." With a moan, she whirled. "Aunt Millicent, how can we possibly arrive at Mr. Jordan's house looking so?"

"Everyone who travels appears disheveled and dirty. That is why a good host always has his guests immediately escorted to a room where they can repair the damage done by their journey." She dabbed at her cheeks with another cloth. "I must say that I believe I shall be a somewhat attractive old woman, if this dusting on my hair is any portent of the future."

Giving her aunt a hug, Bianca laughed. "I suspect you shall be one of those elderly ladies that you de-scribed as old toughs, always speaking your mind and having your way."

"No," Rosie said with a giggle, "you are describing yourself, Bianca. Aunt Millicent is much more re-strained than you are."

"I daresay everyone is more restrained than Bianca." Her aunt smiled and said, "Let us see how much dust we can brush from our clothes. Mistress Innkeeper seemed to think that we had little time before our meal would be waiting."

Bianca savored that moment when they were all laughing throughout dinner. The common room was not large, and only one other table was occupied. The two men, she guessed from their comments, were traveling to London. The large window framed the sea with its diamond mullions, and a fire was waiting to be lit on the hearth whose chimney must be the one that reached up into their room.

The food was not up to Rosie's standards, but the meat had no rot and the vegetables were so crisp Bianca guessed they came from the garden she had seen past the back door. Keeping her attention on her food enabled her to avoid looking at Lucian.

Like them, he had not changed from the clothes he had worn in the carriage. His hands and face were clean, but she had noted wisps of dust still clinging to his hair.

Too often she sensed his gaze on her. It dared her to raise her eyes and meet his. She would not be so jobbernowl, not when her mind was muddled with conflicting longings. She knew she would be a fool to welcome Lucian's kiss again, but she could not forget how wondrous it had been until he had ruined the moment. She should be thinking of nothing but what she would do when she reached Plymouth. Upon their arrival tomorrow, she must devise a way to reach the *H.M.S. Bellerophon* and Napoleon. That was all she should have on her mind, but images of Lucian Wandersee endlessly intruded. His smile, his eyes that promised even more pleasure, his touch which sent quivers of delight along her.

Blast it! If there was to be a match made, it should be between him and Rosie. She could not consider marriage for herself until her final debt to her brother was paid in full. If she had argued more with Kevin, insisting that he consider what would happen to their family if he was killed, he would have remained in Dunsworthy Hall. Instead, she had let herself become enmeshed in his dreams of glory and had not listened to her good sense. She could not be so witless again.

Lucian's laugh forced its way through her invisible cloak of misery. "I saw some tablets of hieroglyphics at Lord Montville's house several years ago. He had them brought back by soldiers and diplomats who have traveled in Egypt, even though we may never know what they say, if indeed the pictures are a language."

Rosie put down her glass and asked in the soft voice she used on the few occasions that she spoke with him, "When you touch the tablets, how did they feel?"

"Feel? May I?" He held out his hand to Rosie, who regarded it with an expression halfway between dismay and terror. Her interest in Egyptian artifacts must have overcome her shyness, because she put her hand on his and let him bring her to her feet. Leading her to the hearth, he ran her hand along the stones on the hearth. "The hieroglyphic fragments feel exactly like that."

"I thought somehow they would be softer," Rosie said as they came back to the table.

He chuckled. "A stone is a stone, although the limestone is a bit smoother than the rocks along this shore. You can see for yourself at Jordan's house."

Rosie glanced at Bianca as if wanting to be certain she was not mistaking Lucian's words, and a smile exploded across her face. "He has some fragments?"

"In his book-room, there were about a dozen when I last called at his house. I believe a larger collection is stored safely at Fortenbury Park, and these are the less valuable ones. I have no doubt that Jordan will be agreeable to letting you touch them."

Lucian listened to Rosie's effusive thanks as she began to prattle as he had never heard her do. While he listened, he watched Bianca's face. She was so protective of her younger sister, something he could understand because she did not want to lose Rosie as she had her brother. Was that why Bianca was seeking marriage for her sister rather than herself? That made little sense, for if Bianca married well, she would be able to provide for both her sister and her aunt. With her alluring wit, beauty, and fiery spirit, she would have many suitors despite her lack of a dowry.

He stood as Bianca and her sister rose, excusing themselves to take a walk in the garden. Although he would have liked to go with them, he could not leave Millicent alone in the common room. A wry grin twisted his lips as he sat again. Despite Bianca's words to the contrary, it seemed he was very much a gentleman.

"That was kind of you," Millicent said. "Rosie has been fascinated by ancient Egypt since she first read about it. To give her the opportunity to see a fragment of those hieroglyphics for herself is most generous of you."

"It was nothing, for I suspect that Henry Jordan will be glad to show the fragments off to someone who is no longer filled with *ennui* each time he or his brother speaks of them."

Millicent held out her glass for him to refill it with wine. As he had before, he wondered why no man had offered for her. Even though her dowry was the obligation of the Dunsworthy children, Millicent Dunsworthy was a comely woman who should have caught many eyes. Her mature beauty was what her nieces would possess in a decade.

"You have succeeded in drawing Rosie out of her bashfulness with this discussion," she said, taking a sip of the wine.

"Mayhap she has come to trust that I mean her no trouble."

"And Bianca?"

"What of Bianca?" he asked, wary at this unexpected turn in the conversation.

"I trust you mean her no trouble as well." She wagged a finger at him. "I see how your eyes twinkle when you look at her when you think no one is watching."

"Twinkle, you say?" He leaned back in his chair. "I thought no male past the age of twelve had twinkles in his eyes."

She laughed. "Mayhap not a twinkle, but a definite glint that suggests your thoughts are upon her."

Lucian picked up his own glass. This sharp insight into the minds of others might have been the reason why no man had proposed to Millicent Dunsworthy. What man would want a woman who could guess the course of his thoughts with such ease?

"Bianca inspires one to think devilish thoughts when one sees the devilment in her smile," he replied.

"Yes, I would say you are two of a kind."

"I must disagree."

"Why?" she asked. "You are both strong-willed as well as passionate about what you believe is right and wrong, and you both have an obvious sense of duty to family. You may not realize that I know, but I saw you give Moss a message as soon as you were hale. You wished your mother to learn you were alive and well." She held up her hand to halt him from interrupting. "Those are just two ways you and Bianca are much alike. Yes, you may have much Town polish and she has spent the whole of her life in daisyville, but that is incidental."

Trying to keep the conversation light, for he did not want it to wander where it should not, he said, "You sound as if you believe that I have the wrong impression of Miss Bianca Dunsworthy and that I should take another look at her."

"No, I am saying I believe you should look at her for the first time." She put her glass on the table and stood. As he came to his feet, she said, "My comments have astonished you. I can see that, and I know it is because you have seen only the Bianca who speaks her mind."

"Yes."

"That is only a façade she hides behind just as Rosie conceals her lighthearted ways behind shyness." Smiling at him, she said, "If you give Bianca a reason to let you past that façade as you have with Rosie, you might be amazed at the woman you will discover there, Lucian."

"Then mayhap it would be for the better that I do not explore beyond that façade." He clasped his hands behind his back so Millicent could not see how they clenched as he said the words he must. "It would not be fair to either Bianca or me."

"That is your choice. I just wanted you to know that you have that choice." She bid him good night.

Lucian sat again and picked up the bottle of wine, refilling his glass. Was Millicent matchmaking, too? He considered her words. If he sought no ulterior motive behind what she had said, Millicent wanted only to ease the rest of their time together. Could things ever be easy around Bianca? She roused strong emotions in everyone she met, whether a deep tenderness in her sister or unexpected admiration in his coachman.

He lowered his glass back to the table. If he intended to show Bianca the dangers of trying to make a match for two people whom she believed to be unaware of her intentions, he must select *her* match with care. He did not want to see her hurt, only for her to understand that manipulating people was wrong.

With a terse laugh, he wondered how he could teach her that lesson when he was doing the same thing himself. He pushed away from the table and stood. His plan was going to take much more thought before he put it into place, and he had less than a day to perfect it.

"I wish I could grow rhododendrons as big as these in our garden," Bianca said while she looked up at the bush that rose higher than her head. It was set beside a wall that separated the garden from the shore and the sea. "With all the trees around the cottage, there is not enough sunshine, I fear."

Rosie smiled. "We could have the trees cut down."

"Then we would be battered even worse by every storm off the sea. I suppose having small rhododendrons is a good exchange for having a warm house in the winter."

"I would say our house has been very warm in the past fortnight."

Bianca turned to face her sister. "What are you talking about?"

"Lucian Wandersee."

"Oh." She was startled that Rosie had brought up his name. Mayhap her plans were already succeeding. "I have noticed that you are much more comfortable around him. Is there a warmth growing between you and him?"

"I was not speaking of me and Lucian, but of you and him."

"I do not wish to speak of him now. I want to enjoy a walk in this garden."

"I thought you found him amusing," Rosie said. "You certainly seemed very taken with him when you two danced that waltz on the green."

"A case of festival fever, as you put it so well."

"Are you certain of that?"

Bianca nodded. "Most certain." Telling Rosie how Lucian's touch had enthralled her would ruin her plans to make a match between Lucian and Rosie. To speak of how he had kissed her . . . No, she would not think of that now, because the memory threatened every bit of her restraint.

"Good."

"What is good?"

Running her fingers through the daisies by the walk edging the garden, Rosie said, "I did not want you to be upset because he asked me to be his partner at dinner tomorrow night at Mr. Jordan's house."

"I shall not be upset." Bianca blinked, for her eyes suddenly seemed heavy. With tears? Impossible! She should be thrilled, for the invitation was another sign of the success of her attempts to make Lucian see Rosie as the perfect bride. Rosie was speaking of him, and he had asked her to be his partner for dinner. So why were her eyes flooded with tears? She wanted to convince herself they were tears of joy, but lying to herself was not a good habit. By the time they reached Mr. Jordan's house, she would have her reaction under control, because, by then, she would have reminded herself of every reason why a match between Rosie and Lucian was a good goal.

"I am glad," Rosie said with a smile. "Lucian said he was certain he could find someone to escort you and Aunt Millicent into dinner. He seems to know so many people."

"The members of the Polite World spend months together in London and then more time together in the country, so they become very familiar with each other."

"Too familiar," said Lucian with a chuckle when he came into view as Bianca and Rosie walked around the large boulder in the very center of the garden. He must have been perched on it, for he was setting himself on his feet. "After seeing the same people day after day and night after night for months, it is refreshing to have new faces and voices joining us."

Bianca wondered how much of their conversation he had overheard. She reminded herself that he could not have been privy to her thoughts, only the innocuous words she had spoken. If he had heard that she preferred admiring the garden to prattling about him, then he might turn his attentions, as he should, to Rosie.

"Did you come out here to look at the stars admiring themselves in the sea?" he asked as he glanced toward the sea beyond the garden wall.

Rosie said, "That sounds like poetry."

"I am no poet."

"Bianca is."

"Really?" He put his foot on the side of the boulder, rested his elbow on his knee, and smiled. "I must own to being surprised, Bianca. However that explains one curious thing. Now I understand why you were disdainful of the poem on the side of the church."

"That silly thing?" Rosie laughed. "Bianca, did you drag him through the high grass to see those silly old words?"

He did not give Bianca a chance to answer. "She most certainly did, and I was quite impressed with the rhyme carved there. Would I be as awed by your work, Bianca? Rosie is, and I assume she is well-versed in verse."

Rosie giggled at his sally, but Bianca said, "I have not written anything since—for several years." She hoped neither Lucian nor Rosie would take notice of how she faltered.

A worthless wish, because Lucian asked, "Since your brother was killed?"

"Yes." She did not slow as she walked into the inn. "If you will excuse us, Lucian, I believe Rosie and I should seek our beds. You said earlier that you wish to make an early start on the morrow."

"I did, but . . ." He smiled at her sister as they reached the base of the stairs. "Rosie, will you excuse us a moment while I speak with your sister?"

"Bianca should not—"

He pointed to the door open to the taproom. "We are standing in clear view of everyone in this inn."

Rosie glanced at her sister. "That is true." She gave Bianca a kiss on the cheek. "Do not be long."

"I shall be up before you know it." She frowned at Lucian, hoping he understood the meaning of that commonplace as well.

He must have, because he said, "What I have to say will not take long."

Rosie climbed the stairs, ducking as she reached the landing.

Bianca watched Lucian as he watched her sister disappear up the stairs. She hoped to see an expression of regret that he had no excuse to ask Rosie to stay. It was not on his face. No matter, he had asked Rosie to go into dinner with him their first night at Mr. Jordan's house, a good sign her plan was unfolding as it should.

She was less sure of that when Lucian asked without any preamble, "Why do you constantly hide your grief from your sister?"

"I do not hide it." She climbed up one step so that as soon as she could escape from this conversation, which was clearly going to be uncomfortable, she would do so.

"Rosie believes you are over your grief."

"I am glad."

"But that is not true." His eyes narrowed. "Or is it, mayhap, that you try to pretend the loss of your brother is no longer important to you?"

She ran her finger along the round ball at the top of the newel post. "You know that is not true."

"I know, but I am puzzled why you act as you do."

"We simply do not speak of our loss often. There is no need when we all miss Kevin horribly."

"Which battle did he die in?"

"None. He sickened with smallpox days after he

reached the Peninsula. Without his family to take care of him, he had no hope of surviving."

He put his hand over hers on the banister. "Bianca, his chances of overcoming smallpox if he had been at home would have been almost as slight."

"I know that, but he might never have contracted the disease if he had remained in Dunsworthy Hall." She clamped her lips closed before she could add, *If I had tried harder to convince him to stay in England.*

"Who knows what might have happened if he had stayed at Dunsworthy Hall?" He stroked her hand gently. "Playing 'what if' will gain us nothing but regrets."

"Is this all that you wished to discuss with me? You could have spoken of these things when Rosie was here."

"But I could not speak of this." He moved closer to the stairs, and she found his eyes, the exact shade of a still, deep pool, were even with hers. "There is a 'what if' I did not want her to overhear."

"What?"

"What if you had not taken me to see that rhyme on the church?"

She stiffened and drew her hand out from beneath his.

"I am sorry my kiss offended you," he said quietly.

"Offend?" She hated how the word squeaked out. "I think it would be for the best if we both forget what happened by the church."

"Can you?"

"I can try. You must as well."

He leaned toward her, and his breath warmed her lips with each word. "I shall endeavor to do as you wish, for that is what a gentleman does when a lady makes a request, but I doubt it will be easy to forget such a sweet kiss."

Fighting the desire to step into his arms once more, she squared her shoulders. "Shall we forget as well how you laughed at me?"

"Not at you, but at us." He smiled. "Bianca, you have taken too seriously something that was meant to be a show of friendship."

She wanted to ask if he kissed other friends with such ardor, but she knew that would be treading on dangerous ground. "I trust you will refrain from showing Rosie such friendship."

Raising his hand, he said, "I vow that if I kiss another Dunsworthy woman on the lips, it will mean far more than friendship."

She was torn between being pleased with his answer and sad that such a kiss would be between him and Rosie. Taking care to duck on the first landing, she rushed up the stairs before her face could betray her once more. When her eyes filled anew with hot tears, she willed them away. On the morrow, they would arrive at Mr. Jordan's house in Plymouth. She finally would be able to find a way to confront Napoleon as she had vowed and ease her aching heart. That was what she needed to think about. No more thoughts of Lucian's kiss—of friendship!—must plague her. She would not allow it. She hoped that was a vow she would be able to keep, too.

Chapter Ten

The city of Plymouth seemed to have grown up out of the sea, curving around the inner harbor and watching over the waves curled up against the shore. Ships clogged the harbor, straining against their anchors in their eagerness to return to some distant land.

Above the cliffs, except for a wide flat park, houses clustered together. The whole city seemed to be on the move, with wagons and pedestrians going to and fro from the docks to the warehouses and into the city.

"Jordan's house is on the far side of Plymouth," Lucian said, "so we should be there within the hour."

"What is that open area?" Bianca asked.

"That is the Hoe." He smiled broadly, and she was amazed how he could act as if their conversation last evening had been completely congenial. She longed to ask him how he hid his feelings, then she wondered if he was hiding anything. If he had been honest, he considered her a friend with whom one could speak plainly.

"The Hoe?" asked Rosie.

"Surely you have heard the tale of how Sir Walter Raleigh wished to finish his game of bowls before sailing out to meet the Spanish Armada. If it is something other than a legend, he must have played them on the Hoe, for the game is still enjoyed there today."

"Can you see the *H.M.S. Bellerophon* from here?" Bianca tried to keep the excitement from her voice.

Her question was a mistake, she discovered, when Lucian leaned to look out the window on her side. His arm brushed against her hip in a most inappropriate way, and fire scorched her. She fought to keep her breathing slow and even. To push him away might cause him to topple and end up in Rosie's lap.

Sitting back, he smiled and said, "I am afraid I cannot pick the *Bellerophon* out from the others from here. I would have to get closer and read the writing on her hull. You understand, Bianca, how much better it is to be able to see something close up."

She paid no attention to his bold glance, which dared her to denounce him for kissing her. Why did he treat Rosie with such gentleness, as if her sister were a porcelain shepherdess sitting on a mantel, while he baited Bianca with every word and expression? Despite his assertion to the contrary, she would not have to meet any other men to know that he was, without question, the most vexing man she had ever met.

"How very kind of you to try!" she cooed.

Aunt Millicent and Rosie stared at her in astonishment, but her pose of righteous indignation was ruined when Lucian laughed and said, "It is a pleasant change to have in my debt for once instead of vice versa."

"If you think a simple query puts me in your debt, you are—"

"Bianca, I suggest we speak of other things," said Aunt Millicent quietly.

Recognizing that tone as one that should never be argued with, Bianca looked out her window again. The soft sound of another chuckle from Lucian added to her irritation. How could she deal with his lack of manners when Aunt Millicent insisted on perfect ones from her?

Bianca never had seen such a large and fanciful house. It had been built to resemble a castle, with its crenellated walls and a huge tower on one corner. She could imagine Rapunzel leaning from one to lower her hair so her lover could climb up to her arms. The windows marched in the neat, precise style of the past century, so she guessed the house was not as old as it appeared to be. Mayhap it would not be as dark and ancient on the interior as Dunsworthy Hall.

But the house's true glory spread out around it. The gardens were multilevel and filled with a variety of plants. She could see how one section of the gardens flowed into the next like a green river filled with bright blossoms. She hoped she would have time to explore these beautiful vistas. They would be staying here for at least three days, so surely she could find a chance to steal away to stroll through the gardens.

Moss stopped the carriage beneath a porte cochere set on the side of the house so it did not ruin the fantasy that this was a medieval castle. The door was thrown open by a footman in pristine, but astonishingly bright blue livery.

"Welcome to Jordan Court," the footman intoned,

standing so stiffly that he could have been a Beefeater.

Lucian repeated under his breath, "Jordan *Court*? Does he think that name will confuse anyone into thinking this is an ancient manor house?" He smiled at Bianca as her sister and aunt were handed out of the carriage by the footman. "Welcome to the *ton* and all its illusions, my dear."

"Don't call me that, please," she hissed.

He chuckled. "Why not? It will allow you to become accustomed to the illusions right from the onset of your visit at Jordan *Court*." He waved the footman away as he stepped out and turned to offer his hand to her. "You will discover that such a term as 'my dear' is not always intended to be endearing. It is often meant to be condescending."

"I thank you for your warning, and I will assume you meant neither." She took his hand and let him help her to the cobblestones.

He did not release it. "I am quite serious, Bianca. You and your sister should heed very closely the cautions your aunt has given you."

"You make it sound as if there will be wild beasts here, ready to tear us limb from limb."

His eyes glittered, but his smile was icy. "Mayhap I exaggerate a bit, but only a bit."

"I know a woman must take care when men are in their cups."

"Lovely women like the Dunsworthy women must take care even when the guests are sober, for your beauty could intoxicate even the most abstemious of men."

"Such words! More flummery?"

He raised a brow. "You are learning Town cant with surprising ease, my dear."

Bianca started to smile, but looked away as she brushed dust from her gown and tucked loose tendrils of hair back under her bonnet. "I doubt anyone would describe us as lovely now."

"To the contrary, you are the pattern-card of love-liness." His finger hooked around one of the strands of her hair and pulled it out from beneath her bonnet again. "To own the truth, it looks better like this." He dropped it onto her nose.

Scowling at him, she turned away and, as she shoved the hair out of sight again, stared up at what appeared to be a barbican at the gate of the castle. Its thick walls were as smooth as a sheet of paper, de-signed so that no enemy might gain a handhold on it. Arrow slits marked where the upper floors would be. At its crenelated top, two flags flew. One was the British flag. The one beneath it was of the same bright blue as the footman's livery, so she guessed the design on it was the Fortenbury family crest. Her awe tempered when she saw a housemaid rush in and come out with an armload of sheets. That incredible building must be the laundry.

"Absurd, isn't it?" asked Lucian, warning her that he was observing her closely.

"You have no romance in you!"

His smile was once again cool. "There is enough romance in England. With Byron and Scott writing their tales of great heroes and breathless heroines, we have been fed that pap until we should be sick of it."

"Mayhap you have, but you do not speak for all of us."

"No?" He stepped in front of her. "Is this silly

façade of romance what you want, Bianca? A poor copy of what is so compelling that it takes one's breath away? Nay, the real sensation is more than that. It is something that grips you so deeply inside that it becomes part of every breath." He took her hands and lifted them up between his own. Curling her fingers over his, he held her gaze with his.

Was he trying to tell her something more with his intense stare? If so, she could not understand it.

He lifted her hand to his lips, but did not kiss it. "This is a greeting that can be used to hide both contempt and desire. Is this insipid imitation of passion all you yearn for, Bianca, or do you wish to experience something far more powerful and devastating?"

She yanked her hands out of his, irritated she had let him lure her near once again with his presumptuous words. Did he talk like this to Rosie? Unlikely, because Rosie would have come to her, distressed by Lucian's presumptuous comments.

As if she had spoken Rosie's name aloud, her sister called, "Bianca, do not dawdle! The footman is waiting to take us to our rooms."

"Excuse me, my lord," she said with a mock curtsy. "I fear I must leave you to puzzle out an answer to your question alone." She did not wait to hear his reply.

"Breakfast is served from sunrise until the clocks chime ten," Mrs. Haggerty, the housekeeper, was saying as she threw open a door. The tall, spare woman's gown was a paler shade of the vibrant blue worn by the other servants, and her apron was a sedate gray. "I trust this will do for you for your nieces, Miss Dunsworthy."

Aunt Millicent peeked inside and smiled. "It shall do very well, Mrs. Haggerty. My room—"

"Is two doors down on the other side of the hallway. I apologize that I could not find an apartment for all of you together, but there are many guests in Jordan Court at the present time."

While Aunt Millicent assured the housekeeper that they appreciated the welcome, Rosie rolled her eyes. Bianca struggled not to giggle. Even if this was not a castle, Mrs. Haggerty clearly ran her household as if she were the chatelaine. Bianca could almost hear the rattle of thick, iron keys that Mrs. Haggerty would have worn dropping on a chain from her waist if she had been walking through a medieval castle instead of through this pleasant house.

"Bianca," Aunt Millicent said, "take your sister in and rest before dinner this evening."

Linking her arm with Rosie's, Bianca went to the open door. She stopped as if she had run into a solid wall, astounded by the sight in front of her.

The room's sweeping ceiling was painted a soft blue that suggested they had stepped outside once more. The walls were covered with dark green silk, and the furniture scattered throughout the room was upholstered in a much lighter green. Doors opened to other rooms. A broad hearth was set opposite a bay window.

She wanted to rush about and explore every inch of the room in the round tower. Exchanging a smile with her sister, she managed to keep her steps slow as she took off her bonnet and set it on a lyre table.

"Lord Wandersee mentioned that you had not

brought any servants with you." Mrs. Haggerty looked down her nose at them, but she was smiling warmly, so Bianca guessed it was a customary expression for the housekeeper. "I would be glad to have a girl sent up for you."

"Thank you," Aunt Millicent said. "That would be greatly appreciated. Rosie, Bianca, I will be back to check on you as soon as I have visited my room."

Bianca hugged her aunt. "There is no need for you to come back here. Why don't you rest? You look so tired."

"That bed last night was as lumpy as a patch of squash." She turned to follow Mrs. Haggerty, then asked, "Are you certain you will be all right?"

"We are going nowhere but within our rooms until you have returned for us." She put her hand over her heart. "I promise."

Aunt Millicent gave them each a kiss on the cheek, then went back into the hallway with Mrs. Haggerty.

When Bianca looked at her sister, she was astonished to see Rosie's smile had vanished. "Whatever can be wrong?"

"The way you promised." Her lower lip trembled. "That is the way you and Kevin always promised to keep a secret. I have not seen you do that since . . . since . . ."

Bianca drew her sister into her arms and hugged her. "Do not be sad, Rosie. You know Kevin would have wanted you to enjoy this weekend." Pushing her sister back far enough so Bianca could look into Rosie's tear-filled eyes, she said, "And you know he would have enjoyed it, too."

Rosie nodded. "He would have. He would have laughed at how overmastered we are by this house."

Abruptly she smiled. "We are to have an abigail. I never imagined that we would have one."

Bianca hugged her sister again. Before Kevin's death, there had been scarcely enough money to maintain Dunsworthy Hall, so they had gotten by with only a handful of the servants necessary to run the kitchens and stables. A lass to look after their clothes and tend to their hair was beyond anything they could have afforded. It was probably for the best, because, when they moved to Dunsworthy Dowager Cottage, they had not missed not having servants.

"Do not become accustomed to such luxury," Bianca said.

"I will not, but I want to enjoy every minute of this."

"So do I!" She took Rosie's hand and walked to the nearest door. "Oh, it is a bedchamber."

Rosie pulled away and opened another door. "And a second one. Come and see this!"

Bianca could not pull her gaze from the bedchamber in front of her, even when Rosie urged her a second time to look at the other room. She stepped into the room, sure she had entered a fairy tale. The walls were the amazing color of mother-of-pearl, like what she had glimpsed within a shell. A fireplace backed up to the one in the other room, and chairs were set next to a window that was draped in chintz decorated with pink and blue flowers.

But what held her eyes was the incredible bed. The beds in the dower cottage were simple rope beds with no carving on the headboards. At Dunsworthy Hall, all the best furniture had been sold to support her father's gambling habits before Bianca was born, so she had never seen anything like this bed.

This bed had a wooden canopy and bed curtains made of the same chintz as the curtains. The white coverlet appeared to be raw silk, and lace edged the pillows, which were propped in front of the headboard, which had been carved by a master craftsmen. The pastoral scene of hills and sheep, which could have been copied from any farm in England, reached to the canopy. She smiled more broadly when she saw what was undeniably Pan playing his pipes to two well-endowed young women, whose Grecian drapes barely concealed their curves.

Rosie rushed in and gasped. "The bed in here is even grander than the one in my room."

"This could be your room if you wish."

"I do not think I could sleep with *him*—" She tapped the satyr, then pulled her hand back and shook it as if something disgusting were on it. "I do not want him leering over my head. My bed has a carving of flowers and trees in an ornate garden."

"Then I will let Pan and his companions keep me company." She went to the windows and smiled at the view of the exquisite gardens. The silver line in the distance was the sea, she realized. Throwing open the window, she strained to hear its whisper, which had been an unending song throughout most of her life. They were too far inland for it to reach her ears.

"Isn't this incredible?" Rosie dropped backward onto the high bed, spreading out her arms as if she intended to make a snow angel. "Dunsworthy Hall must have been like this once."

"This house cannot be even a hundred years old. It was built to be beautiful. Dunsworthy Hall was a fortified house, and nobody cared about frescoes when they had to worry about repelling invaders."

Rosie rolled over onto her stomach, propped her elbows on the coverlet, and leaned her chin on her hands. "That is why I am glad we do not live in Dunsworthy Hall any longer. I never liked that musty, fusty old house."

Sitting on the white chaise longue in front of the window, Bianca began to undo her shoes as she regarded her sister with amazement. "I never knew that you are happier at Dunsworthy Dower Cottage than you were at the Hall."

"Do not misunderstand me. I am sad when I think of the reason we are living at the cottage, because I would have gladly lived in that damp and dark old hall if Kevin could still be alive." She wrapped her arms around herself. "I used to be frightened of the ghosts in the Hall."

"Ghosts? There are no ghosts in the Hall."

"You may believe that, but I am certain that they were there. I could hear them banging things in the tower where Aunt Millicent told us we never must go."

"Storm shutters striking the inner walls are not ghostly."

"And I heard their moans."

Bianca laughed. "That was only the wind off the sea swirling through the broken floors and sliding down into what was left of the tower."

"And I heard footsteps when I went into the tower to see why Aunt Millicent did not want us in there."

"Vermin and birds, I am sure." She stared again at her sister. "*You* went into the tower after we were told to stay away?"

Rosie wore a knowing smile. "I am not always prettily behaved."

"I am glad to hear that." Bianca stumbled on the few

words. She was astonished, and she almost asked what other adventures Rosie had had without her. She did not want to talk about the past. She wanted to delight in being in this wondrous house and this incredible room.

"You will never be able to convince me that the tower was not haunted." With a laugh, she sat and asked, "Did you see that painting on the ceiling in the foyer? Do you think Aunt Millicent would let me paint the ceiling in the foyer of Dunsworthy Dower Cottage?"

"Our foyer is nowhere as grand as the one here." She chuckled. "However, it would give you a chance to paint something other than the pictures of the sea."

She guessed Rosie had not heard her because her sister mused, "I had no idea that anyone painted a ceiling!"

"Or carved such scenes into beds."

Rosie laughed. "And where else do you think they should have carved such things?"

Slapping her sister playfully on the hand, Bianca said, "I trust you will not be so plainspoken when you meet the other guests."

"No." She seemed to shrink within herself. "What if I say the wrong thing and embarrass us all?"

"You? 'Tis more likely that I will not be able to curb my tongue."

A knock on the door heralded the arrival of the maids who would help them dress for this evening's meal. Bianca wondered if her eyes were shining as brightly as her sister's. It was sure to be one of the most exciting nights of her life.

* * *

"Close your mouth, Rosie," Aunt Millicent murmured as they came down the curving staircase to the antechamber of the room where the guests would dine tonight. "One would think you had never been in gracious company before."

"Not in a house like this."

Bianca flashed her sister a sympathetic smile. It was difficult not to stare, gape-mouthed. Each step brought more of the incredible panorama into view. Although she would have liked to pause to look at the paintings in the gallery that ringed the staircase on the upper floor, she had heeded Aunt Millicent's warning that they, as the guests of their host's guest, must not be late. She hoped her best ivory gown and Rosie's best light green gown would be adequate for the gathering. Aunt Millicent was wearing a gown that Bianca had never seen, a silk of a soft pink that matched her cheeks. She carried an ivory fan attached by a ribbon to her wrist. Although Bianca was curious if it was a gown Aunt Millicent had updated from her interrupted Season and how long she had had the fan, she did not ask.

A pair of footmen stood on either side of the arch, which she suspected was broad enough to ride a pony cart through. They bowed from the waist as Aunt Millicent led the way into the room.

In spite of her resolution not to appear to be a bumpkin, Bianca's eyes grew round while she stared at the opulence. A pair of crystal chandeliers were suspended from the ceiling. The light from the candles above made the room as bright as a summer day. An orchestra was playing a lively melody that lilted through the room.

"How beautiful!" she said in delight.

"I thought you would like it," Lucian answered with his irrepressible chuckle. He must have been watching for their arrival.

As she faced him, her breath caught as it had when she saw the grand chandeliers. She had thought that he had dressed elegantly before, but what he had worn at Dunsworthy Dower Cottage had been an understated elegance compared to what he wore this evening. His coat was as black as his hair and unmarred by even a mote of dust. His cravat was tied in an elaborate knot, which was somehow not ostentatious. Silver breeches matched the buttons on his white waistcoat, which was bare of any other decoration. A hint of lace at his cuffs tickled her hand as he lifted it to his lips for a cursory kiss before he did the same for Rosie and Aunt Millicent.

A throat cleared behind him, and he turned. "Ah, here are your escorts for the evening."

A twinge deep in Bianca's stomach refused to be ignored as she recalled that Lucian had asked Rosie to be his dinner partner. She wanted to believe it was excitement that her plan was taking a step toward fruition. She smiled as she was introduced to a Jordan cousin, whose name was Horatio, and to a Wallace, who was the uncle of the bride. If he spoke the uncle's given name, she did not hear it. The Wallace uncle seemed mesmerized by Aunt Millicent, who regarded him with a smile as she tapped her fan in her hand.

Horatio Jordan, who appeared to be a year or so younger than Rosie and had sandy hair that fell forward into his eyes, tried to make conversation with Bianca, but after the usual questions of how her trip to Plymouth had been and the good fortune that the rain had held off until most of the guests had arrived, the silence grew between them. It could not have been more than a few minutes before the doors were thrown open wider so that they could enter, but to Bianca it seemed as if at least two lifetimes had passed.

Lamps were set in the center of each of the score of round tables. Four chairs were arranged around each table. In the corners, potted plants grew in wild abandon, and flowers decorated each table, suggesting that they were dining in a garden.

When Horatio offered his arm with a grace she had not expected, Bianca walked with him into the dining room. He seated her on a chair decorated with petit point needlework. Bianca smiled as Lucian sat Rosie across from her.

Their meal was served by servants who were so hush-footed and skilled that Bianca could have almost believed the food was appearing out of midair. She listened, grateful that Lucian took command of the conversation, while the two men spoke of the last time they had seen each other. They had been hunting quail. As Horatio gave a description of how he had bagged each bird, Rosie ate without speaking. Bianca did say a bit more, but only when Horatio paused to ask her a question before beginning the tale of the next bird he had spotted.

When Lucian pushed back his chair and came to his feet, Bianca looked up, glad for the interruption in the long-winded explanation of how Horatio had skulked up on one bird. A tall man stood beside the table. He was smiling broadly and carrying two glasses of champagne.

"Wandersee," he said as he put down the glasses

and slapped Lucian on the back, "I am glad to see you alive."

"You should not believe all you read in the newspapers." Without a pause, he said, "Miss Bianca Dunsworthy and Miss Primrose Dunsworthy, allow me the pleasure of introducing our host, Henry Jordan."

"Ladies." He bowed over Bianca's hand, then Rosie's. He smiled at Lucian. "I am delighted, as well, to find you in such lovely company, my friend, but I see you have a problem."

"Is that so?"

Mr. Jordan picked up one glass and took a sip. "The dancing is about to begin, and I would not inflict Horatio's dancing upon any of my guests." He smiled and handed the other glass to his cousin. "No insult meant, cousin, but I know how you abhor dancing."

"No insult taken." Horatio drank eagerly.

"Ah, I have just the thing," Mr. Jordan said. "Wait here."

Lucian saw Bianca's eyes narrow. He wanted to tell her that she need not be suspicious of Henry Jordan or of any of this family. They were eager to make each guest's visit a complete delight.

When he saw where Jordan was headed, he said, "Excuse me, ladies, Horatio."

He went to where Jordan was talking to his older brother. Rupert Jordan, Lord Fortenbury, sat at a table with his grandmother. As he came to his feet, he was an impressive specimen. His broad shoulders could have belonged to a farmhand, and his dark brown eyes revealed an intelligence that could daunt anyone in the room.

"Rupert, will you dance with Miss Dunsworthy?" Jordan was saying as Lucian reached them.

The viscount looked across the room and smiled. "The one facing me is lovely. I will be delighted to dance with her."

Lucian followed Rupert's gaze and knew he was speaking of Rosie. He said quietly, "That is Miss Primrose Dunsworthy, although she prefers Rosie."

"Does she?" he asked. "How delightful!"

"Do not be distressed if she does not say much. She is painfully bashful."

"I will endeavor to put her at ease." He walked toward the table, where Horatio was waving his hands as if trying to flush birds out of an invisible bush.

Henry's eyes were wide. "By all that's blue, I daresay I have not heard Rupert speak all day of anything other than how he thinks this party is absurd. Now . . ."

"Now I must ask you to excuse me. There is someone else I must speak with to arrange a dance for the other Miss Dunsworthy."

"But I thought that you would dance with her."

"Not the first dance." Lucian smiled as he walked to another table. "Bullock, just the man I had hoped to see."

The robust man heaved himself to his feet. "Wandersee, you look much better than the last time I saw you."

"I would hope so. How are you faring?"

"Well, thanks to you and the fast attention of the servants at the club.

"I am glad to hear that." He clasped the man's thick arm, then said, "I have not had a chance to tell you how much I appreciate—"

Color flashed up Bullock's face. "Say no more. It is over."

"Allow me to even the debt I owe you." Lucian chuckled under his breath as he recalled saying almost the same words to Bianca. "I am in the company of three ladies this evening."

"Three?" He shook his head. "You must be the luckiest man I know."

"An aunt and two nieces. Fortenbury is dancing with the younger niece. Would you do me the favor of standing up with the older one so I may escort the aunt?" He pointed to where Rupert Jordan was introducing himself to Rosie. "That is the younger sister. The older sister has her back to us."

"If she is half the beauty of her sister . . ."

"I think you should see for yourself."

Walking with Bullock to the table where Horatio was still filling Bianca's ears with his tales, Lucian said, "This is Miss Bianca Dunsworthy. Bianca, my good friend Franklin Bullock."

"How do you do, sir?" He saw surprise and then comprehension in her eyes, which was quickly masked, so he knew she had recognized Bullock's name.

"Much better upon having made your acquaintance, Miss Dunsworthy." His huge hand seemed to swallow her fingers as he bowed over them. Glancing up at Lucian with a smile, he brought her hand to his lips.

Lucian clasped his hands behind his back. All too easily, he could recall the softness of Bianca's skin against his own mouth. He swallowed hard, wishing his glass of wine were closer. He could use a deep drink as he watched Bullock kissing her hand.

"May I be so bold," Bullock gushed, "as to ask you to stand up with me for the first quadrille, Miss Dunsworthy?"

"Do say yes, Bianca," Lucian said, "for I promised your aunt the first dance this evening."

Had his voice sounded as stilted to her as it did to his own ears? She glanced at him and away so quickly that he could not discern her thoughts. He had become accustomed to the heated sparks and the gentler fires within her gaze, each giving him a hint about the thoughts she so seldom could conceal. Now it was as if there were thick walls between them. He had not guessed he would feel such an emptiness when the connection between them was splintered.

"Of course, I would be honored, Mr. Bullock," Bianca replied as Bullock brought her to her feet and offered his arm.

Lucian watched them walk behind the viscount and Rosie, toward where couples were gathering for the dance to begin. His plan to do a bit of matchmaking himself had begun well. So why in the blazes did he find it impossible to smile?

Chapter Eleven

Bianca came down the stairs she had descended last night. There was at least one other set of stairs somewhere in the house, because Mrs. Haggerty had brought them up a different staircase, but she did not want to waste time searching for it.

Last night, while dancing with their host, she had asked if she could have the use of a cart to go into Plymouth. He had assured her that his guests were welcome to use anything the house and stables had to offer.

"Good morning!"

She whirled to see Lucian and Mr. Bullock coming down the stairs with Rosie in tow. Mr. Bullock had monopolized her time last evening. The dance she had had with Mr. Jordan was the only one she had not danced with the muscular man, whose graceful motions had been a great surprise. Her hope that Lucian might ask her to stand up with him when he was not dancing with Rosie had withered away as the night went on. He seemed to stay as close to Rosie as Mr. Bullock did to her.

She had to own that Mr. Bullock was very pleasant company. He shared her interest in flowers, and their conversation about some of the new species that had

been brought from the East in the past few years had
been insightful. If she had not been so distressed that
Lucian did not ask for even one dance, she would
have enjoyed the evening thoroughly. Lucian's
pointed avoidance of her was vexing, but what else
could she expect? And she had seen Rosie's face
glowing with happiness when she danced with Lucian or, on several occasions, with Lord Fortenbury.

"Good morning," Bianca replied, smiling.

"Where are you bound on such a grim day?" Mr.
Bullock grinned, hurrying to her side as if he thought
she might rush away.

"I thought to go and see the *H.M.S. Bellerophon*
where Napoleon is being held prisoner." She tugged
at the kid glove on her left hand. "It was much the
talk at dinner last night."

"An excellent idea. We shall make a party of it,"
Lucian said, offering his arm to Rosie, who smiled
and took it.

"There is no need for that," Bianca said, dismayed.
She might not be able to find a way to get to the ship
if the others were with her. "I mean only to drive past
the shore and—"

"Nonsense," said Mr. Bullock. "You will not be
able to see as well from the road as you will from the
Hoe on the edge of the cliffs. Shall the four of us go
take a peek at Boney?"

Bianca found herself being swept out of the house
like a leaf in a flood tide. As Mr. Bullock asked for
his carriage to be brought, her smile widened. Mayhap this was not a disaster, but serendipity. Alone, she
could not have gone to the edge of the cliffs. Now,
with these companions, she would be able to go to the
shore to discover if there was a way to get across the

harbor to the *H.M.S. Bellerophon*. If she turned the conversation in the right direction, she might even persuade someone else to ask the questions she wanted answers for. That would keep away suspicions of her true motives.

The only one who might see through her ploy was Lucian. Rosie was having too much fun to think of dreadful thoughts like the past war. Mr. Bullock was kind, but he did not know her well enough to guess why she really wanted to visit the shore. With luck, Rosie would distract Lucian enough so he would not take note of Bianca's intentions.

She glanced at where her sister was bumping a small stone with her toe. When Lucian spoke to her, she replied quietly, but with few words. Bianca was astounded. After seeing her sister's happiness last night, she had begun to believe Rosie was putting aside her shyness with Lucian.

She did not need to talk with him while they were dancing. The country dances were not like the waltz he danced with me.

Bianca wished that thought had not invaded her mind, because it brought with it the resonance of the pleasure of being in his arms. So close now to doing as she had promised to do in Kevin's memory, she must think solely of figuring out a way to get onto the ship where Napoleon was being held prisoner. She knew that, but she could not keep from looking again and again at Lucian and her sister.

When an open carriage arrived with a tiger at the back and two men in the box, Mr. Bullock went to talk to his driver.

Bianca said, quietly, "I do not care where the rest of us sit, but Rosie sits facing forward." Her frown warned she would not have her mind changed about this.

"A gentleman," Lucian said with a smile that warned *her* this trip might not unfold exactly as she had planned, "always allows the ladies to sit facing forward when there is enough room." He held up his hand to assist her into the white carriage, which had garishly bright red wheels.

Amusement glistened in his eyes, and she tried to guess what he found funny. When his gaze flicked beyond her, she bit her lower lip to keep from asking him why he had acted as if Mr. Bullock were causing his good humor. Mr. Bullock was his friend. She wondered why Mr. Bullock put up with Lucian, because Mr. Bullock was the epitome of a gentleman, and Lucian's manners could be roguish.

The open carriage had less room than Lucian's closed one. Bianca found little space for herself between her sister and the tooled leather side of the carriage. She was amazed that Lucian could share the other seat with Mr. Bullock's bulk. She tried to shift to give them more space and bumped her knees against Lucian's. Wanting to ask him to move them, she could not because Mr. Bullock sat with his knees apart, and Rosie's legs were drawn back tightly against the seat.

"Comfortable?" Lucian asked cheerfully.

She was not fooled by that effervescent tone, however, when her eyes met his. He knew she was cramped in the narrow carriage, and he was relishing this chance to tease her when courtesy required her to say nothing.

"This is very nice," his friend replied. "Shall we go

and see what has everyone agog in Plymouth harbor?"

Bianca stiffened as each motion of the carriage rubbed her knees against Lucian's. No matter how much she pressed her legs back against the seat or how straight she sat, his knees still bumped hers. He seemed indifferent to the touch, for he was talking with Mr. Bullock about people she had never met.

"I am amazed," Rosie said, "that anyone would act so. Aren't you, Bianca?"

Not wanting to own that she had not been paying attention to anything other than the brush of Lucian's knees against hers, she smiled. "You and I know very little of the ways of the *ton*."

Her sister frowned. "We were talking about a highwayman who was preying on innocent passersby in Hyde Park until he was captured last week."

"Oh."

Lucian leaned back against the seat, a motion that pressed the length of his legs from knee to ankle against hers. "Bianca seems to be thinking of something other than the latest poker-talk from London. Will you share what is on your mind?"

"No, thank you," she said. "I doubt you would find my thoughts at all to your interest." *Or to your liking*.

"Then I will share what is on my mind." Resting his elbow on the side of the carriage, he said, "This is a fine vehicle, Bullock. I should have considered bringing something other than my cumbersome carriage."

"It would have gotten you out of London much faster."

"The carriage did well enough." He laughed. "I have not had a constable chasing me down, so I assume the watch decided to forget about Andover's idea of arranging for such a unique dueling green."

Mr. Bullock frowned. "Such talk is not for these gentle lady's ears."

"These gentle ladies patched me up and saw me through the fever that could have killed me in the wake of that foolish exercise in futility."

"Is that so?" Mr. Bullock gave Bianca a warm smile.

"Quite so," she replied. "We did what anyone would have done." She flinched as Lucian's knees began tapping hers in time with the melody floating toward them from somewhere along the Hoe.

As Rosie turned on the seat to look to her left, where ladies were strolling beneath frothy parasols in spite of the gray skies, Bianca was able to shift enough to edge her knees away from Lucian's. She heard his hushed chuckle. If he thought the whole of this was amusing, he would discover how serious she was when she . . . No, she could not reveal even a hint of her hope that she could find a way to speak face-to-face with Napoleon.

Was she wrong to try to arrange a match for him and her sister? Rosie was such a gentle soul. While she might have a civilizing effect on the rascally Lucian, he could easily hurt her with the wrong word or a sharp laugh. She was amazed to recall that he had never spoken with less than kindness to Rosie. Mayhap that was an excellent sign of his affection for her. Yet, if that was so, his unending teasing would show he had a complete lack of affection for Bianca, and he had kissed her with such passion.

She was confused, a state she despised. Rosie and Lucian seemed to be taking to each other quite well, so staying back and observing might be the best course now. Mayhap by watching, she would understand more about this man who puzzled her endlessly.

The carriage stopped alongside the open green park called the Hoe. Ladies walked by on gentlemen's arms while children ran chasing a ball or a hoop or each other. The bowling green was filled with men trying to best one another. Where the park ended abruptly at the cliffs, a crowd of people were gathered, their backs to the city. She guessed they were looking at the ship where Napoleon was imprisoned.

Her stomach tightened at the thought of being so close to the abominable man. She could not be cowhearted now. Napoleon was a British prisoner. He would not be allowed to harm any of them again, and this weekend would be her lone chance to tell him of the pain in her heart, a grief shared by too many here and across the Channel.

Taking Mr. Bullock's arm, Bianca tried to pay attention to his comments about the plants they passed along the walkway. She would have been fascinated if she were not in such a hurry to get to the cliffs to see the *H.M.S. Bellerophon.*

"'Tis not a race," Rosie said, panting, as they turned to walk toward the sea. "Do slow a bit, Bianca."

Only then did Bianca realize how swiftly she had been leading them across the Hoe, with the tiger in his bright blue livery and the man who had been sitting beside the coachee in tow. Slowing her steps made every muscle ache, because she longed to propel herself with every possible bit of speed in her to the far side of the Hoe.

Bianca gripped the stones on the seawall as she

pushed through the crowd, determined that no one
would budge her from the edge of the cliff until she
had seen all she wished. Several ships were anchored
in this section of the harbor, but the *H.M.S.
Bellerophon* was the only warship.

She stared at the ship that was moored closer to the
shore than she had imagined. Even with its sails
furled and its sheets bare to the sky, it had an undeniable dignity. Was it eager to be on its way to some
distant island to rid itself of its odious passenger?

Astonishment made her gasp when she saw small
jolly boats being rowed out into the harbor. They were
set in an arc around the *H.M.S. Bellerophon* as people ogled the ship. Where were they hiring the small
rowboats? It must be on the beach below.

Seeing people on the walkways that followed the
curve of the cliff and dropped toward the shore,
Bianca said, "I would like to go down to the lower
level."

Mr. Bullock hesitated. "The walkway is steep. Do
you think that is wise?"

"It is too steep for me," Rosie added. "I shall stay
here, but go if you wish, Bianca. I know seeing the
ship is something you have been very anxious to do."

Bianca glanced at her sister, who was regarding her
with a sad smile. Somehow, Rosie was privy to things
Bianca had not told her. Hiding her plan to do more
than peer at the ship would be difficult, but she must.
Rosie was certain to go to Aunt Millicent to prevent
Bianca from reaching the *H.M.S. Bellerophon*.

"I am going down," she said, motioning to the tiger
to accompany her. "You may wait here for me."

"You cannot go alone." Lucian held out his arm

when Mr. Bullock did not reply. "I will walk down with you."

"Be careful, Bianca," her sister said.

She nodded. She would be careful, although she doubted Rosie realized that Bianca was more concerned about being alone with Lucian now than she was about the steep walkway. Then she smiled. Being alone would be impossible. Not only would Mr. Bullock and Rosie be watching from above, but there must be a score of people along the walkway and even more on the shore. As well, the tiger would trot after them like an obedient puppy.

"Shall we?" Lucian asked.

"Yes, thank you." She ignored the challenge in his voice as she tucked her hand into his arm. If he thought she would let her vexation with him override her determination to find a way to get aboard that ship, he was sadly mistaken.

When she gripped his arm more tightly as they descended to the lower walkway, Bianca had to own she was glad she had not come alone. Falling down would be ignominious and dangerous.

"Steady," Lucian said with a laugh. "A tumble from here would land you in the water, if you are lucky. If not, you could strike the rocks."

"It is steeper than I thought."

"But you would have come down here, no matter what, wouldn't you?"

She met his eyes without flinching as she spoke the truth coming directly from her heart. "Lucian, you know how important this is for me."

"Yes, I do." All humor vanished from his voice. "I hope seeing this ship and knowing Napoleon can never escape his captors again will help diminish

your grief." He paused by the seawall along a flat section of the walkway. "I think you will have the very
best view from here."

Bianca agreed as the tiger moved several paces beyond them to give them privacy to talk without him
overhearing but still close enough to act as a watch-
dog. She was tempted to tell the lad that he need not
worry, because Lucian seemed quite taken with her
sister, and Bianca had come here for a reason that had
nothing to do with a flirtation.

Scanning the shore, she saw two men below sur-
rounded by a half-dozen smallboats. Lines gouged
into the shore showed that other boats had been
beached there. Those must be the boats bouncing on
the waves near the *H.M.S. Bellerophon*. Watching as
a trio of men handed some coins to one of the boat-
men, she smiled. The men on the shore were renting
the boats.

Her first impulse was to ask Lucian to take her out
in a jolly boat. She silenced that thought. Even if she
persuaded him to do so, and it was unlikely he would
agree, she was certain he would not take her close
enough to the ship so she could board it.

"You seem disappointed," Lucian said.

"I guess, in a way, I am."

He laughed tersely. "I know you would prefer if
Boney were imprisoned in a prison hulk with water
leaking through the boards and rats stealing his food."

"No, I am not interested in that sort of vengeance."

"Then what sort?"

She put her hands on the seawall and watched as
another jolly boat was pushed into the harbor, carrying even more gawkers. "I would like him to know
the depths of the suffering he has caused and for him

to accept that blame. If he no longer believes those sacrificed lives were worth the cost of building an empire, then surely he will be haunted by the grief the rest of us have endured."

"Whew," he said, arching his dark brows. "Your sort of vengeance is far worse than imprisoning him in a prison hulk. What you are suggesting—that he acknowledge every death is his fault—would drive most men mad."

"He is not most men. He is intelligent and, I hear, as charming as you, Lucian."

"I would rather you not use me as a comparison for anything you have to say about that dirty Corsican," he said with sudden sharpness.

She put her hand next to his on the seawall, then boldly placed it atop his hand. When he tore his gaze from the ship to meet her eyes, she said, "Forgive me, Lucian. I know that you are among those who have suffered from his wars."

"I have put those memories behind me when I left the Continent after I thought my duties were finished with his banishment to Elba." His voice became a growl. "What widgeons we were to think he would not have allies on that island so close to where he was born!"

Pushing back from the seawall, Bianca looked down at where people were crowding the lower section of the narrow walkway to stare at the ship. "Have you put it all behind you? Is that why you fretted about being too late when you were lost in your fever?"

"What makes you think that something I said in the midst of a fever had anything to do with the war?"

She did not answer as he seemed abruptly mesmerized by the *H.M.S. Bellerophon*. For several long minutes, he remained motionless. She said nothing, for she needed him to answer the question. His answer might give her further insight into the man she was hoping would marry her sister. As she regarded his stern profile, she bit her lip to keep from saying that she wanted his arms to enfold her and hold her close to his strength.

When, as if shaking off the cloak of dank memories, he looked at her, she saw the pain of thoughts he had always kept hidden before. She could not imagine what he might have endured in the war and what he might have done to survive it.

"It was not what you said," she whispered, "but the expression in your eyes. The grief returns each time I mention the words you spoke during your fever. What happened, Lucian?"

"It is nothing I should speak of to a lady."

"Or anyone else?"

"Who would want to listen to words coming from a fever-maddened man?" He rubbed his hands together as if they were icy cold.

She took them between hers, not caring how the people walking past them stared. Lucian needed to understand what she had come to understand. "Whatever is within you is festering just as the wound did in your arm. You will never be fully healed unless you relieve its pressure within you."

His eyes narrowed, and he opened his mouth. He closed it as he looked skyward. "I believe we should leave now. The walkway is becoming choke-full of gawkers, and it is beginning to rain."

A drop hit her nose, but she did not want to let this

conversation come to such a quick, unsatisfactory end. "Lucian, I would listen if you wish."

He said nothing for a very long minute, then murmured, "I know you would." He cupped her cheek for a moment, then jerked his hand away and frowned at it as if his fingers had disobeyed him. "But we must leave now."

"Lucian—" She bit back what else she had been going to say when his scowl refocused on her. Hearing laughter and cheerful conversations around them, she wondered if he was right not to become mired in grief. They could not change the past, even though it would always remain a part of them. Forcing her voice to be as lighthearted as the others, she added, "I hope Mr. Bullock's carriage has a top that can be raised, so we are not drenched."

"I trust it does." Lucian drew her hand in within his arm again. Walking away from the people pointing at the ship and whispering as if Napoleon could hear them from wherever he was imprisoned in its cabins, he led her up to the top of the cliff.

Bianca looked toward where her sister and Mr. Bullock had been standing. They had wisely already left to return to the carriage. The rain was falling harder with each passing second.

When they reached the Promenade, Bianca looked in both directions. "There," she said, pointing to where the carriage now sported a brilliant red roof to match its painted wheels.

He pulled his coat off and handed it to her. "This may keep you a bit drier."

"Nonsense, Lucian. Now you will be soaked."

"We both shall be soaked if we stand here and have

yet another brangle instead of running to the carriage at our best speed."

That Bianca could not argue with. Holding the coat over her bonnet, she hurried as quickly as she dared on the wet walkway to the carriage. Lucian handed her in as she warned her sister and Mr. Bullock to take care they did not get wet, too. When Lucian was seated, Mr. Bullock gave the command to go.

Finding herself staring at the firm muscles beneath his wet clothes, Bianca held Lucian's coat out to him. He shook his head as his gaze slowly slid along her. She looked down and saw that her wet gown was clinging too closely to her.

"Thank you," she whispered, as she shoved her arms into the sleeves that hung down past her fingertips. Wrapping the coat around her, she made herself small against the seat.

He smiled, not the rakish one he used to unsettle her or the knowing one aimed at infuriating her. She was unsure what this smile meant, but she was very sure of its effect on her. A warmth within her grew until she wondered why steam was not rising from her wet clothes.

She was grateful Mr. Bullock kept up a steady patter all the way back to Mr. Jordan's house. By the time they reached it, the shower had vanished. It must have been a fickle one, because the driveway was dry and the sun was peeking through the clouds.

Rosie hurried Bianca into the house to have a warm bath before she caught a cold. Looking back, Bianca was caught by Lucian's eyes. The distance between them vanished as she saw the sorrow he could no longer hide from her. If he yearned to put that grief behind him, he must confront it as she must confront Napoleon. She wondered if he could.

Bianca walked through the most formal garden among the dozen surrounding Jordan Court. Over her head, she carried a parasol that would offer little protection if it began to rain again. However, the sky was an eye-searing blue and provided the perfect backdrop for the flowers. She had come here to escape the aimless conversation the ladies were sharing. Talk of weddings and trousseaus and dowries for people she did not know held no interest for her, so she had excused herself.

She paused to admire some flowers planted in the center of a diamond created with well-trimmed boxwood. If Mr. Bullock were with her, she suspected he could identify the flowers she had never seen before.

A bush on her left rattled, and Bianca paused. When Lucian pushed through a narrow opening in the tall hedge, she asked, "Are you following me?"

"Do not flatter yourself." He looked over his shoulder. "I am fleeing from Bullock. He insisted that I join him for a stroll through the gardens so he could give me a dressing-down for being so careless as to forget about watching the sky for rain and endangering you."

"I was in no danger from raindrops."

"That I know, but Bullock seems to have cast himself in the role of your protector."

Continuing along the path made of broken shells, she said, "He is a very pleasant gentleman, who shares my interest in flowers. I owe you a thank you for introducing us."

"I thought you might find him interesting, and he is searching for a wife."

"Wife? I have known the man for barely a day. Do not have me betrothed before I have had more than two conversations with him." She did not pause before adding, "In spite of what you profess, you did not happen upon me by chance, Lucian. That is not your way."

His smile became chilly. "You are right. When I could escape from Bullock with promises of never endangering you in any way again, I saw the top of your parasol over the hedges. I thought I would come and ease my curiosity."

"About what?"

"About your fascination with that filthy Corsican."

She put her hand up to brush the leaves of the ivy that had almost consumed the opening to a pergola, concealing it in a lush coat of green. "You could see today by the crowds gathered around the harbor that my interest in the man is not uncommon."

"It is for you."

"What do you mean?"

He cupped her elbows and turned her to face him. "I may not have known you long, Bianca, but the experiences we have shared have shown me facets of you that you might not have revealed otherwise. Although you act prickly, you have a gentle heart focused entirely upon your family. Because of that fact, I know this obsession with Napoleon must have something to do with your family."

"You are right. It does, but why are you asking me about this? I told you that I wanted to see the ship where Napoleon is imprisoned to help me ease my grief over Kevin's death."

"You cannot expect me to believe that you are satisfied with a mere glimpse at the ship."

"Believe what you wish." She drew her arms away and walked along the wall to where the stairs led to the lower formal garden. Going down them, she started to follow the wall back toward the house. She yelped in astonishment when Lucian jumped off the wall, landing right in front of her.

He straightened, adjusted his dark blue coat, and gave her the iciest smile she had ever seen. "No," he said when she tried to edge around him in the sparse space between the wall and the boxwood hedge. He plucked her parasol from her fingers and leaned it against the wall. "You are not going to use some weak, silly excuse and a show of being affronted to avoid this discussion that is long overdue."

"I owe you no explanation."

"No, you do not owe me an explanation. However, I thought you might want to give me one." His hands curved along her shoulders and down her arms. Weaving his fingers through hers, he smiled again. This time, his expression was a sad one. "Bianca, I do not know what burden you are toting about on your slender shoulders, but I am offering to help you bear it."

She would not let his kind words woo her into doing something skimble-skamble. "Why? Don't you have enough to carry on your own shoulders? You do not wish to share any of that with me. Why would I ask you to share my own most private emotions?"

"I wish to help you."

"Then go and take Rosie to see the fragments of hieroglyphics you said Mr. Jordan has here."

"I intend to show them to her before dinner. Right now, I am talking to *you*. You did save my life."

"For which you have repaid me by bringing me and my family to Plymouth."

He drew her hands up and pressed them against his chest. "Do you honestly think such a huge debt could be recompensed by a mere offer to ride in my carriage on a journey that I was already taking?"

A taut voice replied, "It would be best for everyone if you got back in that carriage and left, Wandersee."

Bianca started to turn toward the voice, but Lucian's hands tightened on hers. When she winced, he released her. She looked over her shoulder and saw a man she had never met. His hair was nearly the color of the red wheels on Mr. Bullock's carriage. Not tall, he wore a frown. As she faced him, she saw a bruise that was fading on his chin, and his nose had a lump on its top as if it had been broken. He stepped closer, slapping a newspaper against his hand.

"I did not realize that Jordan had invited you," Lucian replied.

Bianca flinched at the loathing in his voice. She had never heard him use such a rancorous tone.

The man held up the newspaper. "Did you think I would let you slander me like this, Wandersee, and do nothing?"

"Slander? I have said nothing about you that is not true."

"Shall we obtain another opinion on this?" He shoved the newspaper into Bianca's hand.

"Do not involve Miss Dunsworthy in your folly."

"Why not?" fired back the man. "Do you fear that her opinion will be in contrast with yours?" Jabbing his finger at the newspaper, he said, "Right there, Miss Dunsworthy!"

Bianca looked down at the page. It was the *Morning Chronicle*. She gasped when she noted the date on it was the same as the edition that Lucian had shared with them in the carriage. Seeing the gossip printed on the page and noting how Lucian's name jumped out from almost a dozen places in the column, she realized this must be the page he had claimed was missing. What had he been trying to hide from them?

Lucian snatched it from her before she could read the specifics of the gossip. Crumpling it into a ball, he tossed it at the other man's feet.

"Unlike you," Lucian said coolly, "I do not embroil a lady in my business. If the truth has become identical to slander, then I have no choice but to plead guilty to the charge."

The man bristled. "I still await my satisfaction."

"If so, you shall have to wait a great while longer."

"Name your friends!"

Lucian gave a terse chuckle. "You know my friends, and you know that I will not involve them in any duel to satisfy your absurd pride that has not been bruised by me, Andover."

Bianca drew in her breath with a gasp. Andover? Was this the man who had instigated the asinine duel and shot Lucian? That would explain his broken nose and the fading bruise on his chin. Her fingers curled against her palm. He had almost killed Lucian, first by shooting him and then failing to stop Lucian from leaving London without medical care. Both could have meant Lucian's death.

A blinding fury erupted within her. Although she knew she should remain silent, she could not keep herself from saying, "Lucian might have died after you forced him into doing something stupid. He is too smart to become ensnared in such a confrontation again."

"Bianca," Lucian said softly.

She ignored him as she scowled at the man in front of her. "If you always act so out of hand, you should blame yourself for your tarnished honor. Your comments are contemptible."

"Who is this woman?" Andover asked, his indignation blazing in his eyes. "Your convenient, Wandersee?"

"Stow your jabber." Lucian's voice became a low growl. "I will not allow you to insult Miss Dunsworthy, who, with her sister and aunt, saved my life when I stumbled upon their home, sick with leaden fever brought on by the ball fired by your gun."

"So you own to having her at your bedside, but not in your bed." He laughed with contempt. "Either you are lying, Wandersee, or you are not man enough to take advantage of this country lass, who has enough intelligence to take advantage of *you*."

"No one is taking advantage of anyone," Bianca retorted, "save for you, who are taking advantage of our good manners to spout your venom, Mr. Andover."

"*Lord* Andover!"

"Then you have even less of an excuse for such churlish behavior." She knew she was overstepping the bounds of propriety to speak so to a peer, but even if she had wanted to, she could not stop the words that tumbled past her lips. "A gentleman would not have used the tactics you did to force another man into a duel. If an untitled man acted as you did, he would be sent to Tyburn and the hangman."

When Lucian began to laugh, Lord Andover's scowl became even darker as his face reddened to the shade of his hair. He jabbed his finger at Lucian. "Do you allow this dog's lady to fight your battles for you?"

Lucian's laughter vanished. He grabbed Andover's lapels. "Do not speak so of Miss Dunsworthy, Andover. You are the whelp of a cur, not her." Shoving the man back several steps, he added, "If you continue to show a want of manners, I vow I shall teach you some. The lacing will not be one you soon shall forget." He drew Bianca's hand within his arm. Picking up her parasol, he handed it to her. "Let us go. I have heard all I wish from this widgeon."

Andover sputtered behind them, but did not follow. Bianca resisted the temptation to look back and give him a superior smile. When she heard Lucian snarl a curse under his breath, she put her other hand on his arm.

"He is not worthy of your anger," she said quietly.

"What he said about you—"

"Is untrue." She gazed across the perfect garden toward the house, its dozens of windows sparkling in the sunlight. "One of the advantages to having no title, Lucian, is there is no need to defend its prestige. I know what and who I am. It does not matter to me how I am judged by someone who does not know me."

"You are a remarkable woman." He slipped his hand over hers.

"No." She laughed. "I simply do not want to have to patch you up once more. You were, without question, the most impatient patient I can imagine."

He paused and brought her to face him once more.

"Our conversation that Andover interrupted is not over. Bianca, I know you are not satisfied with a single look at Napoleon's prison. What do you plan to do now?"

"Do not ask me anything else."

"Why?"

"Because I vowed always to be honest to you, Lucian, and I do not want to have to break that vow."

"You know I will try to stop you from doing anything that could put you in jeopardy."

"I know." She hurried back toward the house before she could tell him that not even he—or the way her heart pounded when he was near—would halt her from speaking with Napoleon.

Chapter Twelve

Lucian was checking his cravat in the glass when there was a knock at his door. Not waiting for the man serving as his valet to open it, Lucian smiled when he saw Bullock in the hallway.

For once, Bullock's coat was not straining across his chest. He was dressed with an elegance Lucian had never seen him assume. For Bianca? That was most likely, and it would mean that Lucian's plan to find Bianca a match before she found him one might be succeeding far beyond his expectations.

His smile wavered. Why wasn't he feeling more of a sense of triumph?

"Andover is here," Bullock said as he came into the room.

Andover could be the reason he could not exult in his victory over his game with Bianca. Grimly, he said, "I have already had the so-called pleasure of speaking with him."

"And?"

Lucian readjusted one side of his cravat. "Why are you even asking? You know I have an aversion to dueling and other foolish attempts to bolster a man's bloated sense of himself. I will not allow Andover to put me into a situation again where he can precipitate a duel."

"I thought you should know he is saying—"

"No need to repeat what he is spouting off behind my back, for I suspect it is very close to what he said to my face. Letting him upset you is ridiculous, Bullock. I will give you the same advice I gave Bianca. Ignore him."

"Miss Dunsworthy?" His eyes widened.

"I encountered her in the garden before we had the ill fortune to meet Andover on his quest to prop up his battered pride."

Bullock rubbed his freshly shaven chin. "Ah, now I understand."

"What do you understand?"

"It is nothing you have not already heard, I suspect." He smiled broadly. "Let us speak of other, far more pleasant matters."

"Miss Dunsworthy?"

He nodded. "She is an amazing woman, Wandersee."

"I have said so myself on more than one occasion." He pulled on his black coat and settled it over his silver waistcoat.

"So why are you not pursuing her yourself instead of introducing me to her?"

Lucian took his gloves from his valet. Drawing them on, he chuckled. "I am Miss *Rosie* Dunsworthy's escort this weekend. As you have seen, the Dunsworthy women know their own minds, and trying to deal with more than one at a time would prove I was as witless as Andover claims. Shall we join the others?"

Bullock continued to sing Bianca's praises as they went down the formal stairs leading to the hot and stuffy ballroom in a separate wing of the house. Mayhap that was why Lucian saw Bianca first among the crowd of guests in the room decorated with gilt and mirrors on the walls and more frescoes on the ceiling.

Or mayhap it was because she had never appeared as beautiful as she did tonight. Her white dress was the perfect complement to her golden-red hair, arranged à la Sappho, so the curls framed her face. Lacy mitts accented the slender line of her fingers, he noticed, as she pressed one hand to her simple bodice while speaking to someone he could not pull his gaze from her long enough to identify. He admired her with a slow and appreciative look that slid from those endearing curls and along her lovely face and then across her breasts and to the very tips of her slippers that peeked from beneath her gown.

He heard Bullock saying something to him, but the words were lost in a buzz that rushed through him as if a hundred bees were swarming around him, keeping him from hearing anything but that sound and the sudden pounding of his pulse. When every inch of him responded to viewing every inch of her, he swallowed roughly.

With a silent curse, he jerked his eyes away from the far-too-appealing sight of her. Was he mad? She might be beautiful, but she was also outspoken and focused on something that had to do with Napoleon. Even her concern for her sister's well-being ebbed when she was focused on the ship holding the dirty Corsican.

Was she seeking to *help* Napoleon? His lips tightened along with his hands, but he forced his fingers to uncurl, and he banished the thought that she might be trying to aid the fallen emperor. The loathing in her voice when she spoke Napoleon's name was sincere.

As was the craving within Lucian to hold her. He was striding toward her before he had time to form another thought.

Bianca sensed rather than heard Lucian approaching. She turned and met his commanding eyes that suggested so many things she did not dare to believe. As his gaze roved up and down her, she knew she should tell him to stop gawking at her as boldly as the people had at the ship. She could not utter a word, not wanting to ruin this moment when a smile grew across his lips, adding to the fire in his eyes. That flame lit something deep inside her, something that urged her to step forward and let his arms envelop her as he kissed her again.

A fan tapped her arm sharply, and Bianca blinked, letting his dangerous magic sift away as Aunt Millicent greeted him and Mr. Bullock. Mr. Bullock? Bianca had not even noticed that he stood beside Lucian until now. As Mr. Bullock bowed over Aunt Millicent's hand, then hers and Rosie's, she fought her yearning to look back at Lucian and become lost in the craving for his touch.

"Ah," Aunt Millicent said with a laugh as the orchestra set high in a gallery curving around the ballroom began to play, "that sounds as if it will be a waltz. Mr. Bullock, I hope you will not consider me too brash when I say I would appreciate the chance to get to know you better during this dance."

Mr. Bullock's smile wavered for a moment as he looked at Bianca. When Mr. Bullock offered his arm to Aunt Millicent at the same time Rosie slipped hers into Lucian's, Bianca took a step backward.

What an air-dreamer she was to think that Lucian's thoughts had been of her! He may have stared at her, but his attentions now were focused on Rosie. Knowing that she should be thrilled for her sister, she stood and watched as Lucian twirled Rosie about the room. Bianca closed her eyes and swayed to the music, recreating the dance they had shared on the village green. His strong arms, his broad chest, the brush of his legs against hers as his fingers stroked her back with the tempo of the music. Or had it been the tempo of her heart as she lost it to him in that one dazzling moment? Her eyes popped open, but she could not ignore the thought that would remain silent no longer. How could she have been so foolish? A matchmaker must never fall in love with a man she was matching up with another woman.

A dowager pushed through the crowd to watch the dancing. Bianca backed away another step. The gray-haired woman peered at her through a quizzing glass.

"You are the sister of that girl dancing with Lord Wandersee, aren't you?" the dowager asked.

"Yes." She was afraid to say more because sobs might burst from her.

"They are a handsome couple." The dowager wafted her fan, but it could barely move the heavy, humid air. "What an odd match! Your family's unfortunate past would be quickly forgotten when its future is connected to the Wandersee fortune."

"I have no wish to forget my family's past, either the unfortunate or the fortunate parts."

"But think of how wondrous it would be to have this dance lead to a betrothal and a wedding."

Bianca did not answer or bother to excuse herself as she turned and inched back through the press of the guests. She went toward a door leading out to the white garden. Grumbles followed her, but she did not care a rap about impressing the Polite World tonight.

She cared only about what she would do if Lucian offered for Rosie and her sister accepted. To have him be a part of her life but never to be able to hope for another chance to be in his arms was a torment she could not have imagined even an hour ago.

Rushing down the steps into the garden, where every blossom was the same color as her white gown, she kept going until the music from the ballroom faded into silence. She sat on a stone bench and looked at the rising moon. The flowers around her were drooping in the heat, for the sea breeze had vanished, and, although the moon was coming up, the day's warmth rose from the stones of the path.

She clung to the silence, using it to hush her own thoughts. She did not want to think. She did not want to move. She did not want to feel. Not now, not ever again. Folding her hands in her lap, she looked down at them. There were no answers for her when she had been an utter fool.

Bianca was unsure how long she had been sitting there, trying to think of nothing, when a shadow crawled over her. She raised her eyes from her clasped hands and was startled to see her sister.

"What are you doing out here?" Bianca asked.

"Much the same as you, I suspect. Getting some fresh air." Rosie sat on the bench beside her.

"I did not think you would want to miss a minute of the dancing. You looked as if you were having so much fun." She hoped her sister did not hear the taint of desolation in her voice.

"It has been glorious, Bianca. Exactly as I had hoped it would be if we ever had the chance to join the *ton* for a grand assembly, and the dancing allows me to be among these people without having to think endlessly of something clever to say." She smiled. "And I got to see a few of Lord Fortenbury's Egyptian stones this afternoon. They were wonderful, Bianca. I had so many questions."

"You?" She tried to laugh, but could not.

"Yes, *me*. I was excited to see them. I fear Lord Fortenbury must believe me to be a prattle-box."

Bianca touched her sister's flushed face. "He seems to be a very nice man."

"One of the nicest I have ever met. He does not act as if my questions were an imposition. In fact, he has offered to lend me some of his books about Egypt and hieroglyphics."

"I am glad you are enjoying yourself."

"And aren't you?"

Lying to Rosie was inconceivable, so she said, "I have never experienced anything like this."

"How could Aunt Millicent have turned her back on this excitement to take care of us?"

"You would do the same."

Rosie dimpled. "I would like to think so, but this is fun!" Coming to her feet again, she said, "You are right. I do not want to miss a moment of it. Will you walk back in with me?"

"Go ahead. I want to look at those flowers beyond the statue of a milkmaid." She pointed to her right.

" 'Tis not like you to avoid everyone. That is usually me."

"Tonight, you have gentlemen to dance with you and talk about what interests you, so you do not have to worry about being shy."

"That is true." She bent and kissed Bianca's cheek. "Look at your flowers, if you must, but hurry back in.

Mr. Bullock was seeking you. I did not tell him that I suspected you would be here."

"Do not tell him now either. I do not want him to think I am avoiding him."

"Then who are you avoiding?" Rosie asked, her voice abruptly serious.

"You silly goose!" Bianca set herself on her feet, glad the thin moonlight hid how labored her smile felt. "I told you that I wished to look at some flowers, and that is what I plan to do. After I have, I will come back inside."

"As long as there is nothing else keeping you out here."

"What else could it be?"

For a long minute, Bianca feared Rosie would answer that question and reveal that she knew the real reason Bianca had scurried out here. That would be unbearable, because she did not want her sister to set aside her own happiness simply because Bianca had fallen in love with the man pursuing her sister.

Then Rosie gave her a wave and hurried back up the steps to the ballroom, her skirt fluttering after her like soft wings.

Bianca went in the opposite direction to where stairs led up to a higher level of the garden. In astonishment, she realized that, from here, she could see the city of Plymouth and the harbor. The moon's milky path reached from the shore toward a low bank of fog, where the ship with Napoleon must be hidden. Her feet longed to carry her along that road of light, but she knew it was only an illusion.

Leaning her arms on the wall, she sighed. Meeting Napoleon was what she had come to Plymouth for, not to flirt with Lucian Wandersee. She gauged the distance from the house's gate to the city. Not much more than a mile. Had she become so accustomed to the luxury of riding in a carriage that she had given no thought to walking to the harbor?

"You have discomposed Bullock completely," came a hushed voice from behind her. As she turned, Lucian smiled. "He believes you have thrown him over for some other gentleman, and both of you are trying to make yourself scarce."

"Please express my apologies to him as soon as you return to the ballroom." She rested her arms on the wall again and stared at the cloud of fog. Why had Lucian come out here? She could not retain her faltering hold on her emotions when he was close. Mayhap if she gave him terse answers as Rosie had, he would return to the ballroom. Only because Bianca had insisted had he spent any time with Rosie at Dunsworthy Dower Cottage. A serrated laugh sliced into her throat, but she did not let it escape.

"That sounds," he said as he leaned one elbow on the wall, "as if you are trying to rid yourself of *my* company as well."

"Not really." She knew he was staring at her, so she kept looking at the mist.

"Is that more of your honesty?"

"Yes, and I honestly thought you would be dancing with Rosie."

"I was, but I noticed you were not there watching over her as you customarily do. So I left her dancing with Fortenbury, who was babbling to her about those Egyptian tablets of his, after she told me where I might find you."

"Rosie told you that I was out here?" Her anger at her sister vanished as quickly as it had surged forth.

Rosie had promised not to tell Mr. Bullock where Bianca was; she had said nothing about talking to Lucian.

"Yes."

"Oh."

"Is something amiss, Bianca? It is not like you to retreat from any situation."

"The smoke from the gentleman's cigars was bothersome."

"Where they are smoking is a goodly distance from the ballroom."

She laughed as she faced him. "You never allow me the kindness of pretending to accept what I tell you at face value. The truth is that the smoke was bothersome when I came out on the terrace, so I decided to explore the garden. Then I came here and found this splendid view of the harbor."

"Which does not explain why you left the ballroom."

"Do you truly believe that I owe you any such explanation?"

He moved nearer to her. "Ah, that unquestionable honesty again. Tell me something, Bianca. Honestly."

"What?"

"Why are you honest about everything but what you truly feel deep within you?"

"Some things I prefer not to share." Her voice softened to a whisper as he closed the distance between them. "It has nothing to do with honesty."

"It has to do with trust. Trusting someone, for I doubt you allow even your sister or your aunt past this façade you have built with blunt words."

"You have said this before."

"But you have never given me an answer."

"I don't know if there is one I can give you." Tears filled her eyes as the words came directly from her heart. "Why are you asking me this when you hide so much of yourself from everyone, too?"

"From everyone but you, I see. How is it, do you suppose, that we are privy to aspects of each other that no one else is?"

"I don't know." She raised her eyes to meet his gaze. "Do you?"

When his hand curved around her nape, he drew her to him. Her breasts pressed against his hard chest. Imprisoned by the sensations that swirled through her, stripping away every thought but the thrill of his touch, she put her hands on his muscular arms. His arms encircled her waist, and she gasped as he pulled her even more tightly against him. This was what she had dreamed of, being in his arms again, having him kiss her again . . . having him laugh at her again.

"No!" she cried, ripping herself away from him.

"No?"

"I know you consider yourself irresistible to females, Lucian Wandersee, for you have beguiled my aunt and my sister with your nothing-sayings."

His brows arched as he rested one hand on the wall. "Your grasp of the cant of the *ton* has expanded, I see."

"Do not try to change the subject. I will not be part of your *à suivie* flirtations."

"Another bit of slang I did not know you knew." He slid his hand along the wall, so it was behind her. If he closed his arm, he would be drawing her up against him again.

"I do not want you holding me," she lied. Every word was bitter on her tongue, but she would not let this man who had left her sister aglow with happiness now try to woo her into his arms. Her stomach twisted. Was he as faithless as Lord Andover had accused him of being?

No, she did not believe that. He had kept his pledge to repay her for saving his life.

"Lord Wandersee?" asked a footman who appeared out of the shadows like a phantom. "Mr. Bullock is seeking you."

"Tell Bullock that I will be with him directly." As the footman went back toward the house, Lucian asked, "Will you let me escort you to your aunt, Bianca?"

"I think I would rather stay here and look out at the harbor awhile longer."

"Then I will let your aunt know where you are."

"Thank you." She was sure even strangers would speak with more emotion than was in their voices now.

When Lucian walked back toward the ballroom, which glittered like the gems worn by the ladies within it, Bianca closed her eyes. It did no good, because she could not shut out her sorrow. Surrounding her like a haze, it filled every breath she took. Lucian had not denied that he was dallying with her—*and with Rosie!*

She opened her eyes as she frowned at the moonlight. She could not let her sister be led astray as she had been by Lucian's well-polished, well-practiced words. Rosie's heart must be protected from this rogue. Her breath caught in a half sob when she realized she would have to be honest with Rosie about her own infatuation with Lucian, so that Rosie would comprehend the depth of Bianca's consternation.

She stepped away from the wall. Delaying might make the circumstances even more painful for Rosie.

She must go to her sister now and persuade Rosie to heed her.

Bianca walked along the garden path as quickly as she dared, for it was draped in thick shadows. She faltered when she saw a man on the steps leading up to the terrace outside the ballroom. Her heart clutched. Could it be Lucian? Was he waiting for her, hoping that she had changed her mind?

The man stepped down from the stairs and into the moonlight. Her wish shattered when she saw his broken nose shadowing his cheeks oddly. Lord Andover!

"Good evening," she said, gathering up her skirt to climb the steps.

He caught her arm. "Where is your lover, Miss Dunsworthy? I thought Wandersee would keep you under his protection at all times."

"Both Lord Wandersee and I have told you that you are mistaken in your assumptions about our relationship." She tried to pull her arm out of his grasp, but he refused to release it. Astonished, she knew that Lucian must have let her go when she drew out of his arms, for he was stronger than this blustering man. "Please take your hand off my arm, my lord. I wish to return to the ballroom and the festivities."

He laughed. "A fine speech when Wandersee is twirling about the room with your sister. Has he cast you off in favor of her?"

"Casting me off is impossible when we are no more than friends."

"Your protests grow tiresome."

"Then do not let me keep you from seeking other entertainment, Lord Andover."

He tugged her toward him. "But *you* are entertaining in so many ways, Miss Dunsworthy."

"A compliment I am afraid I cannot return." She peeled his fingers off her arm by digging her nails into his hand. When he yelped, she edged away. "I must ask you to excuse me, for I have no wish to linger here any longer."

Seizing her arms, he put his face close to hers. The odor of whatever he had been drinking made his breath sour.

"Release me!" she ordered with every bit of dignity she could find. "Release me, or I shall—"

"What? Scream?" He laughed. "It would do you no good, Miss Dunsworthy. We are still a distance from the ballroom, and the music is loud within it. You picked the perfect place for an assignation."

"I did not come here for an assignation, most especially not with you." She tried to pull away, realizing he would not be reminded of the limits of civility.

"With Wandersee?"

"I told you—Never mind! My private life is none of your bread-and-butter, my lord. Now release me at once!"

"Listen to the country miss giving orders like a fine lady." He laughed again and yanked on her arm.

Pain seared it as she tried to pull away. He was too strong. She drew in her breath to scream. Before she could, he pressed his mouth over hers.

Her reaction came directly from instinct. The crash of her palm against his face matched the sting reverberating toward her elbow. Andover snarled a curse, then grasped her by the hair. She moaned as pins scattered around her. As he bent to kiss her again, her hand rose.

Broad fingers caught it, and she cried out in desperation.

"Allow me the pleasure, Bianca, of giving him another facer."

"Lucian!" she gasped as she was plucked from Andover's arms and shoved aside.

She watched, her hands over her mouth to keep in her scream as Andover swung at Lucian. He ducked beneath Andover's wild fist, then drove his own into Andover's stomach. As the baron bent over, grasping his middle, Lucian's fist slammed into his face. Andover collapsed and did not move.

"Mayhap," Lucian said, staring down at the senseless man, "the third time is the charm for knocking some sense into your hard head."

When he turned and looked at her, she threw her arms around his neck and pressed her face against his shoulder. She did not weep. She was too angry for that. When he caressed her back as she had dreamed of him doing, she whispered, "How dare he think he could treat me so coarsely!"

"Bianca, this is my fault."

"Your fault?" She stepped away from him, although she did not want to leave his embrace. She tried to push her hair back into place, but too many pins had been lost. "I know Lord Andover has tried to incite you to meet him on the dueling green again."

"*This* would have been the best reason he has given me for doing so, but I have no interest in being a target for him again when he is foxed." He caught her face in his hands and tilted it up to meet his shadowed eyes. "Don't you understand? His plan tonight was not to infuriate me, but to ruin you."

"Why?"

Lord Andover groaned and shifted on the ground. Taking her hand, Lucian led her up onto the terrace at the edge of where light spilled from the ballroom. They would appear to be shadows to those within, but she could now see his face. It was lined as if he had aged a score of years in the short time since he had left her in the garden.

"I thought to give you a taste of your own match-making scheme," he said, "but I had no idea Andover would be unable to see that my attempts to make you a match with Bullock were just a jest."

"Matchmaking scheme?" She released her hair, letting it drop over her shoulders as she stared at him.

"Like the one you had to make a match between me and your sister."

"You know of that?"

"Yes."

"How long have you known?"

"Since the first day you arranged for an obviously reluctant Rosie to go for a walk with me. I thought to give you a bit of your own medicine by matching you up with someone here. I chose Bullock, because he is always a gentleman. Unfortunately, Andover took it upon himself to intrude in the game."

She sat on a bench that was the twin of the one in the garden and folded her trembling hands on her lap. "I should have guessed that you invited us here only to make us the butt of your jest. I should have listened to my instincts and told you that we would not come here with you, that we would find an inn closer to the harbor."

"Bianca, to humiliate you is not the reason I invited you here."

"You are lying. Why are you lying to me now when you have been honest enough to own to your scheme?"

He paused for so long that she feared he had gone mute, then he said, "I don't know. Shame, I guess, for treating you so poorly when you saved my life. I never intended you or anyone else to be hurt. You were having so much fun with your matchmaking game, I thought I would have a bit as well. If Andover had not intruded, you would have had a pleasant weekend with Bullock. I never intended to hurt you."

"Thank you for being honest with me about that, if nothing else." Coming to her feet, she said, "You are right. I was trying to make a match between you and Rosie, because I know she wants more than the simple life we have at the cottage. She is pretty and gentle-hearted and will make some lucky man a splendid wife."

"That is true."

"However, her gentle heart is sure to be broken if she learns that her introduction to the *ton* was done to ridicule her."

"Ridicule her?" His eyes widened as he shook his head. "That was never my intention."

She raised her chin with what remnants of pride she had left. "Mayhap you do not remember the poem on the wall of the Dunstanbury church, Lucian. What is inflicted upon one Dunsworthy is inflicted upon all of us. You planned to embarrass me with the help of your friend. How do you think that would have made Rosie and Aunt Millicent feel?"

"It was no more than a jest, and you seemed to enjoy Bullock's company."

"Please make my apologies to Mr. Bullock. If he asks why I have not returned to the ballroom, I trust you will be as honest with him as you have been with me." Her breath snagged on the thick tears in her throat. "Please say nothing to Rosie. Do not break her heart, too."

"Break her heart? Too? What are you saying, Bianca?" He reached for her, but she moved away.

"I am saying good evening, my lord." She walked toward a side door that would allow her back into the house without the disgrace of having to walk through the ballroom in this state.

Footsteps beat the terrace behind her, and Lucian stepped in front of her. "Bianca, don't leave."

"I cannot see any reason to stay. Can you?"

Again his answer was slow in coming. Quietly, he said, "Not one that you would heed now."

"We would appreciate the use of your carriage and Moss to take us to an inn."

"So you are not leaving Plymouth yet?"

Her heart pumped more swiftly when she heard the hope in his voice. Telling herself not to be silly, for she could not trust him any longer, especially with her heart, she said, "I have not done what I came here to do."

"You have seen the ship where Napoleon is cached."

"Yes . . . Yes, I have." She could not let her longing to be in his arms cause her to be want-witted in every way. She must take care what she said. Blurting out the truth now would ruin any chance of her speaking to Napoleon. "But I still have something I need to do."

"Something for which you do not need my help?"

"I need nothing more from you, my lord. Not ever." She walked past him and into the house before the tears scorching her cheeks would show him how she was lying.

Chapter Thirteen

"Did you have a wonderful time during this gathering, too?" asked Rosie as she closed her smaller bag and set it by the door for a footman to take out to the carriage.

"I am not sure that 'wonderful' adequately describes it." Bianca fingered the ribbons on her bonnet. How could she have allowed Lucian to distract her from the real reason she had asked him to bring her and her family to Plymouth? She would not allow that to happen again.

"Isn't it amazing that Miss Wallace has asked us to attend her wedding at Fortenbury Park, the Jordan family seat, next month? I cannot believe how our lives have taken such an exciting turn." She rushed into her bedchamber to gather up the rest of her things. Her joy flowed back in the silly song she sang.

"Neither can I." Bianca looked out the window, which offered a view of the city and the sea in the distance. Her plan to leave Jordan Court yesterday morning and find an inn closer to the harbor had been halted by Aunt Millicent, who could not understand why Bianca seemed so eager to leave this luxury. Aunt Millicent might have agreed, if Bianca had revealed the truth, but telling of how Lucian had played her for a fool was too devastating.

So they had remained at Jordan Court, and Bianca had discovered how easy it was to avoid Lucian when he must be avoiding her as well. He had gone riding with Mr. Jordan and his brother, Lord Fortenbury. That Rosie had told her, and Bianca could not bring herself to ask which man had informed her sister of that.

She had seen Lucian at dinner last night, looking even more dashing and urging her heart to melt as it teased her to go to him and beg him to let them start anew. She could not. His smile had tempered when he glanced in her direction and then away, acting as if he were dismissing her as a problem he wanted out of his life.

Her hands clenched on the windowsill. The carriage would be brought around in less than two hours, and Moss would be taking them back to the dower cottage. Even Rosie did not seem to know if Lucian was traveling with them or remaining here longer. In less than two hours, she probably would not have to worry about Lucian. Not ever again.

Tears flowed into her eyes as they had so often in the past day. She dashed away the pair of teardrops that overflowed. She had been foolish to think he would be unaware of her fumbling attempts at matchmaking.

"But I wanted Rosie to be happy," she whispered. "You were thinking only of yourself."

She must think solely of herself now, for in less than two hours she would have lost her chance to make her dream of telling Napoleon of her pain come true. This morning, at breakfast, Mr. Bullock had mentioned that another ship, the *Northumberland*, was arriving in Plymouth to take Napoleon to distant St. Helena, for the *H.M.S. Bellerophon* was not seaworthy enough to make the long voyage. She must do what she had come here to do.

If she failed at that, too, she was unsure how she could glue her shattered life back together. That might no longer be possible even if she spoke with Napoleon. She had not realized how much a part of her life Lucian had become until he was no longer in it. She had no idea how to fill the void that remained.

Whirling away from the window, Bianca went to the bed where her bags were half packed. Letting her pain with Lucian consume her would keep her from doing what she had come to Plymouth to do. She picked up her best bonnet and her reticule. The few coins she had saved to buy new lace to refurbish gowns for each of them must surely be enough to rent a jolly boat.

She tied her bonnet under her chin as she walked toward the door. She was opening it when Rosie asked where she was going. Closing the door again, because she did not want anyone to overhear and watch where she was going, she hid her reticule behind her back as she said, "I want to take one last walk around the formal garden."

"But we are leaving soon!" Rosie dropped the clothes she was carrying onto the bed.

"It shall not be a long walk." She smiled. "You finish your packing and mayhap rest a bit now, and I shall be back soon. I have an errand I must tend to."

"With Lucian?"

"No, not with him."

Her voice must have been too filled with anger because Rosie halted as she was about to place a chemise in her bag. Facing her, she asked, "Bianca, what is wrong? Have you and Lucian had a brangle?"

"You know how he is." She forced another smile. "He can be more than difficult at times."

"With you, but I think that is because he has a *tendre* for you."

"Listen to you and your cant. You could easily be mistaken for a member of the *ton*."

Rosie stamped her foot against the floor, startling Bianca. "You are trying not to give me an answer."

"I did not hear you ask a question."

"I believe Lucian has a *tendre* for you. What do you think?"

Bianca drew on her gloves and picked up her parasol, which she had not intended to take with her into the city. "I believe if Lucian has a *tendre* for anyone, it is for himself."

"What a cruel thing to say! He speaks endlessly of you, even when it is clear you two have vexed each other again and again."

"I am sorry if my comment upsets you, Rosie, but I try to be honest all the time."

"Then why won't you be honest with me about Lucian?"

"I thought I just said—"

Rosie stamped her foot again. "Dash it, Bianca!"

"Do not let Aunt Millicent hear you speak such language."

"Dash it, Bianca!" she shouted. "Why won't you own to the truth that you have a *tendre* for Lucian just as he has one for you?"

Bianca shook her head. "I have told you that he

does not have any such feelings for me. Mayhap for you."

"Me?" Rosie stared at her, openmouthed.

"He has been very attentive to you since we arrived here."

"Mayhap because he knew no one else would listen to his endless comments about you." She frowned. "He does not have feelings of anything but friendship for me. He has told me so himself, and I have said much the same to him. But when he looks at you, his longing is so clear I swear you should be able to see right to the very depths of his heart."

"That might be true, if he had one."

"Bianca!" Her sister's voice was filled with astonishment. "How can you say such a thing?"

Kissing Rosie on the cheek, she said, "I shan't be long. Take care."

Rosie called something after her, but Bianca walked swiftly along the hallway and down the stairs. She sought a corridor that would take her to a side door. With the many guests milling about the front foyer as they took their leave with the end of the gathering, she did not want to chance being stopped for any reason.

This time, she would do what she had promised herself to do the day they received the news of Kevin's death. She would not be stopped again.

"Stop it!"

"My lord?"

Lucian waved the valet out of the room. That he was talking to himself was bad enough, but he did not need to be talking to himself when there was a servant to overhear. Mayhap he had taken a knock in the cradle, but he could not blame his current state on madness.

He was not mad. He was miserable. He had never guessed he could be so miserable. Even with Andover gone, he was miserable. Andover must have slunk back to London where he could nurse his broken nose and seek some sympathy from those who would listen to his tales.

Bullock had spoken no more than a grunt to Lucian yesterday while the gentlemen gathered to go for a ride along the hills overlooking the sea. This morning, at breakfast, Bullock had stood up and walked out of the room when Lucian entered. Bullock had not said anything, but there was no need. Somehow, the truth of Lucian's jesting attempt to make a match for Bianca with Bullock in reprisal for her matchmaking had spread through the guests, for half the other men now pretended that he did not exist.

Being ignored was not what had made him despondent. It was the other men who came up to him, slapped him on the shoulder, and lauded him for his hoax, which had played itself out with such excitement when the gathering was becoming rather dull. They laughed at Andover's continuing failure to see that Lucian was his better at fisticuffs, and they had chuckled about how Bullock had been parading around the house like a peacock because pretty Miss Bianca Dunsworthy, whom Lucian had introduced him to, seemed so taken with him.

Bianca had been right. Lucian's attempt to even the score between them had heaped humiliation on her and her family. He was, he feared, no better than Andover, who had sought a scapegoat to appease his despair at his mistress's wandering eye. How Lucian had prided himself on being the brave war hero who always chose the proper path! In his search for something to challenge him amidst the *ennui* of yet another assembly with the same faces and gossip, he had brought shame to the Dunsworthy family.

Jordan had spoken with him alone, telling him that Jordan's fiancée had forged a friendship with the Dunsworthy women. This contretemps had distressed Miss Wallace so much that she had asked Jordan to mention to Lucian that staying away from their wedding might be a good idea as the three Misses Dunsworthy were invited.

Lucian would have been furious at the suggestion he was not welcome among old friends, if he had not known it was a reasonable request. He had made a muddle of everything and had hurt Bianca, who had been only trying to make him and her sister happy.

And *that* was why he was miserable. He had repaid her kindness of saving his life by adding more sorrow to hers.

"Fool," he muttered under his breath. "Ingrate."

"My lord?" asked his valet, sticking his head out of the other room. "Did you call me?"

"No . . . Wait, yes!" Lucian stood. "Get me my hat and gloves. I believe I shall check on my carriage."

The valet nodded, disappeared, and returned almost instantly with Lucian's beaver hat and his gray leather gloves.

Thanking him, Lucian went out of the room. Moss seemed to have an objective eye, so mayhap the coachee would have some advice for Lucian before Moss returned the Dunsworthy women to their home while Lucian rode to his estate on a horse borrowed from Jordan. It would not be the first time Moss had helped him out of a difficult situation, and Lucian trusted his coachman's insights into those around them.

At the bottom of the stairs opening onto the corridor that would take Lucian to the door closest to the stables, Lord Fortenbury was pacing as if waiting for someone. The viscount took one look at him and frowned.

"Wandersee," he said coldly.

"Fortenbury." He started to walk past him, then paused. "I should express my regrets at not being able to attend your brother's wedding next month."

"Thank you for letting me know you are otherwise engaged." Fortenbury's lips turned down in a scowl. "Engaged? Engaged in unsavory mischief? That is the crux of the matter, isn't it, Wandersee?"

"I would rather not speak of the whole ignoble matter."

"If you do not speak of it, you are the only one." He turned on his heel and walked away down the corridor.

Lucian wanted to call that Fortenbury was wrong. One other person was not talking about it. Bianca would say nothing for fear of bringing more pain to her family. He frowned. He had heard no mention of the matter when the ladies were present. It might be that only the men knew. No, Miss Wallace apparently knew if she had requested that Lucian stay away from her wedding. None of this made sense . . . unless the other female guests were trying to protect the Dunsworthy women. He doubted that could last long, because someone was sure to let the story slip while drinking too much of Jordan's wine.

"Lucian, are you going out?" Rosie came down the stairs and smiled at him. She was beautiful and delightfully lighthearted, and he knew everyone had expected an announcement to be forthcoming. Yet, she was not the woman who haunted his thoughts . . . and his dreams. "I am glad we have had a chance to speak with you before we leave."

That she was smiling told him Rosie must have no idea of the stories being whispered among the men. He looked up the stairs when he heard other soft footfalls. Millicent! He waited for recriminations, which he deserved, to be fired at him.

Instead Millicent said, "It has been such a pleasure to make your acquaintance, Lucian." She smiled, and he saw, as if never before, the resemblance between her and her most contrary niece. "Thank you for giving us the opportunity to enjoy a visit to Plymouth with you and your friends. It has offered my nieces an insight I could not otherwise offer them into the vagaries of the *ton*."

He bowed over her hand, curious if she was being sarcastic or sincere. He hoped it was the latter, but he wondered how long before the kindness in Millicent's voice became acrimony because he had involved her niece in the bumble-bath he had created so witlessly. "You are very welcome," he said. "I have enjoyed it as well." *Most of it,* he amended silently, so he would not have lying to Millicent added to his list of transgressions.

"I suspect you have." She tied the ribbons of her bonnet with its blue feathers. "Bianca is not here waiting, so, Rosie, will you check that she has not returned to your rooms?"

"Of course, Aunt Millicent." Rosie hurried up the stairs.

"Bianca must be saying adieu to our hosts, although I have no idea what is taking so long. We will be seeing them again next month." She picked up the small bag she had been carrying. "We will be seeing you as well at Fortenbury Park for the wedding, I assume."

He forced his innocuous smile to remain in place. "I am afraid not. A conflicting matter has compelled me to offer my regrets to the groom."

"That is too bad. I know Bianca and Rosie would have been very happy to see you again. I don't know what whim of fate sent you to our house on that stormy night, but you must agree that it was a benevolent whim."

"More than benevolent. Fortunate would be closer to the truth." Now he could be completely honest. "I know I would not be alive now, if it had not been for your household."

"For Bianca. She shouldered most of the responsibility for your care." She put her arm around Rosie's shoulders as her niece came back down the stairs alone. "This one swoons dead away if blood flows anywhere near her, so most of her help was in the kitchen."

"Aunt Millicent!" Rosie chided, her face reddening.

"Do not be embarrassed," Lucian hurried to say. "I have seen grown men faint at such a sight."

Rosie and her aunt exchanged uneasy glances, and he cursed silently. He did not want to distress this whole family before he took his leave of them. *Mayhap you do not remember the poem on the wall of the*

Dunstanbury church, Lucian. What is inflicted upon one Dunsworthy is inflicted upon all of us. Bianca's voice, filled with hurt, echoed in his head like the aftermath of cannon fire.

Rosie looked both ways along the hallway. "Where is Bianca? She was not with Miss Wallace and Mr. Jordan. They have not seen her since last night."

"She was not in your rooms?"

"No," Rosie said, guilt in her downcast eyes.

"You probably saw her most recently, Rosie," Lucian said. "Did she say where she was going?"

"For a walk in the gardens." She faltered, then went on. "But that was almost two hours ago. She did not come back to help me finish our packing after she took her bonnet and parasol." She gulped and looked at her aunt. "And her reticule, which she tried to keep me from seeing."

"You said nothing of this earlier." Millicent frowned.

Rosie's face fell even farther. "I knew you would be distressed if she went for a walk alone in the gardens after what took place there with Lord Andover."

"Andover has already left for London," Lucian said, knowing that he must speak the truth when Bianca was nowhere to be found, "so you need have no fear that she will come to harm with him."

"Again," said Millicent, her mouth a straight line. "Rosie, did I hear you correctly? Did she take her leave almost two hours ago?"

"She kissed me on the cheek and told me to take care." Her eyes grew round. "Oh, my! Do you think she has gone off on her own beyond the gardens?"

Lucian ran out the door. Hearing Millicent calling to him, he paused.

"Where are you going?" she asked.

"I thought she might be in the white garden. It has become Bianca's refuge."

"She will not be in the gardens. I am sure she has left the grounds." She rubbed her hands together. "She thinks that I have forgotten what she said when she wept inconsolably the day we learned of Kevin's death. She repeated the words over and over."

"What words?"

" 'He must know what he has done to so many.' Over and over she said it."

"He? Who?"

"Napoleon Bonaparte."

He could feel the color vanish from his face. "Do you mean to tell me that she has gone back to the harbor alone?"

"Yes, and if I know Bianca, she is determined to speak to Napoleon. Nothing will stop her."

He put his hands on her trembling shoulders. "I shall try."

"It has been two hours. She may already have gotten herself into a mess she will not be able to extricate herself from." Tears ran down her cheek. "But try, Lucian, please try."

"I will." He hoped she did not hear the gloom in his voice, but Millicent knew as well as he all the perils awaiting Bianca in her foolish quest to speak her mind to the most dangerous man in Europe.

Chapter Fourteen

Bianca counted out the coins the man renting the boats was demanding for the use of the rickety-looking jolly boat. At the same time, she tried to keep her bonnet from being snatched off her head by the wind coming off the water. She could have bought the makings for a week's worth of meals for what he was charging for this boat. What choice did she have but to pay it?

He pocketed the coins, then looked up at the sky. "Miss, there be a storm comin' in. May'ap ye should wait till tomorrow."

"Tomorrow may be too late. I have heard that Napoleon is being transferred off the *H.M.S. Bellerophon* as soon as the *Northumberland* arrives to take him to his island prison."

"Ye don't say?" He grimaced. "There goes any more chances t'line m'pockets with a bit more silver."

She gave him what she hoped was a sympathetic smile. Tying her bonnet ribbons into a double bow so they would not be loosened by the wind, she asked, "Will you shove me off from the shore?"

"Do ye know 'ow to row a boat, miss?" His concern refocused on her. "'Tis 'ard to pull against the tide, 'specially when the wind's blowin' in from the sea as it is now."

"I know how to row." She did not add that the only time she had ever been in a boat was on the calm, shallow pond behind Dunsworthy Hall, and Aunt Millicent had insisted that Kevin always accompany her. Kevin! She could not forget the promise she had made to him. Squaring her shoulders, she said, "I shall be fine. Thank you for your concern about my well-being."

" 'Tain't yer well-bein'. 'Tis m'boat's that worries me." He looked at the sky again. "Keep an eye on the 'orizon, miss. A blow is comin' up."

Bianca shaded her eyes beneath her bonnet, for even with the scudding clouds, there was a glare off the sea. She looked at the gray line where the sea and the sky met. It was darker than it had been even moments ago. Her common sense shouted for her to stay ashore, but she would not listen to it now. If she had listened to it in the dower cottage or at Jordan Court, she would not have come here again.

"I shall watch the weather closely." She stepped into the boat and set her parasol beside her on the seat, for she could not hold it and row. Then she put it beneath the slat that served as a seat. She did not want it ruined by the salt spray that would stain the silk. Picking up the oars, she almost gasped. She had not guessed they would be so very heavy, so much heavier than she remembered from her boating excursions at Dunsworthy Hall. Then, realizing that stronger oars were needed in the harbor than on the pond, she said, "If you will give me a push from the shore, please."

"Are ye sure this be wot ye wish t'do?"

"I have paid you what you asked. Now please allow me to use the boat as I see fit."

He pushed back his cap and scratched his head. Then, with a shrug, he bent to shove on the bow of the jolly boat. It ground against the sand and broken shells before it floated free.

The waves threatened to drive it back onshore, but Bianca pressed the oars against the water. With the very first stroke, her shoulders and back protested. She ignored the pain as she ignored her good sense pleading with her to give up this foolish attempt.

Once past the line where the waves were breaking on the shore, the rowing became easier. After what seemed like a half hour, she looked over her shoulder at where the *Bellerophon* was anchored. She groaned. It did not seem any closer, although she was moving farther from the shore. Raising the oars out of the water, she decided to catch her breath.

"What is happening?" she gasped when the boat continued to move out toward the open water. She must have ventured into an undertow, which was pulling her from the shore far faster than she could with her rowing.

She smiled. This was a stroke of luck she had not expected.

Her smile disappeared when a wave washed over the side of the boat, drenching her feet and parasol. "Dash it!" she muttered. She reached down for her parasol, but choked as another wave swept over the side, splashing her face with cold water.

Picking up the oars, she began to row again. She did not want to let the undertow carry her past the ship, but she would take advantage of it for as long as she could. Other jolly boats bounced on the water.

Her heart thudded against her breastbone as she realized that they were much closer to shore and heading in that direction.

Bianca turned on the seat and looked at the horizon. It had vanished into a gray maw devouring the sea. She should turn back, too.

"But this is my only chance," she whispered. "I promised myself that I would do this for Kevin."

As clearly as if her brother sat beside her, she could hear him say, "Don't be silly, Bianca. Think with your head just once, will you, instead of your heart." How often had he said that to her? He had said it enough times that, when he began with "Don't be silly," she would say the rest of the admonition before he could.

She lifted the oars out of the water again and tried to balance them as the boat rocked. The wind scoured her face, and she turned her head, so her bonnet took the brunt of its force. Water soaked the back of her dress. Not from the waves, but from what was being carried on the wind. Risking her life like this was not what Kevin would have wanted her to do. He had gone to fight the French, so that Napoleon's armies would not arrive on the English shore and endanger his sisters and aunt.

She sighed. It seemed that grand gestures were a habit with their family. She would return to shore and pick up the shards of her life with her sister and aunt. Next month, they would be traveling to Fortenbury Park. Who knew what might happen there?

And Lucian . . . She did not want to think of what she would say when she saw him at the wedding. Mayhap she would not have to worry, because he might remain as angry as he had been since their last conversation in the garden. She closed her eyes and imagined his face as it came closer to hers in the moment before he had kissed her by the church. An emptiness within her seemed as broad as the sea, and she wondered how one retrieved one's heart once it had been hopelessly lost to someone who did not want it.

She gasped in horror as a wave broke over the back of the jolly boat, raising the water in the bottom over the tops of her slippers. Another wave lifted out of the trough. She tried to turn the jolly boat, but the wave struck it, tearing one oar out of her hands. The boat rocked madly. She gripped the seat and shrieked when the other oar vanished overboard. Now she had no control of the boat.

She heard shouts. Over her shoulder loomed the dark breadth of the *Bellerophon*. The irony that she had reached the ship when she had been trying to get back to shore was something she had no time to think about now.

More shouts came from the deck above, and she saw the waves were flinging the jolly boat ever closer to the *Bellerophon*. If the two collided, she could be awash or worse.

Spray lashed her as she picked up her parasol and tried to use it as an oar. The handle broke on her second stroke. Tossing it into the water, she looked to her left and screamed as a wave arched out of the sea. It seemed to hang at an impossible angle, then burst over the back of the boat. Water flooded the boat. She scooped out what she could, but her efforts were futile.

Every bone jarred when the jolly boat hit the side of the ship. Bouncing back from the hard oak, the jolly boat whirled about in the waves. More water filled the boat. She heard men calling from above her, but she did not look up. She tried again to bail out the boat.

"Watch out!" came the clear shout from the deck.

Bianca raised her head and cried out in horror as a wave, higher than any of the others, swamped the back of the boat. The stern vanished as the water came up to swallow her as well.

Salt stung her eyes while she tried to figure out where the surface was. The water was the same gray in every direction. She had to find her way up to fresh air and get away from here before she was struck by the jolly boat or the *Bellerophon*.

She tried to claw her way to the surface. How deep down had she been driven by the wave? Or was she beneath the crest of a wave now? How could she survive this sea that had been enraged by the incoming storm?

Hands caught hers and tugged. She kicked her feet and followed them. As her head broke through the surface of the water, she saw a young, freckled face in the second before a wave crashed over her. The hands refused to let hers go, and she clung to them.

"This way," the lad bellowed as she pushed her head above water again. He motioned with his head toward the ship.

Bianca tried the best she could to copy his strokes, but the undertow was trying to pull her past the ship. He pressed a rope into her hands, and she gripped it with all her strength. He grasped it as well. Mouthfuls of water threatened to choke her as they were dragged to the side of the ship.

A rope ladder was unfurled down the side. Although she was unsure if she would be able to climb it, she knew she must. She edged up it, trying to balance herself against the motion of both the ladder and the ship. When she was most of the way up, more hands reached out and lifted her off it and onto the deck.

Sinking to sit on the rocking deck, Bianca took deep breaths. Air had never tasted so sweet. She raised her head as she heard cheers. The lad was climbing onto the deck through an opening between the rails.

"Thank you," she tried to say, but her voice was little more than a croak.

He picked up the cap he must have tossed aside when he jumped in to rescue her. He tipped it to her as another man came forward and held out a glass.

She did not look at him as she took it and drank gratefully. The sweet wine warmed her and eased the sickness in her middle.

"Can you stand, miss?" asked the man in front of her. An ensign, she knew, by his insignia.

"I believe so."

He offered his hand to bring her to her feet. "Are you hurt, miss?"

"No, just drenched."

He drew off his jacket and set it on her shoulders. Shouting an order for someone to bring a blanket, he said, "You should have known better than to come out in this rough sea."

"I had to . . ." Bianca looked past him to see an unmistakable man coming up the companionway.

Napoleon Bonaparte wore the uniform he had created when he became a general. Even though two men flanked him, the aura of power in his dark eyes had not been lessened, not even by his defeat at the hands of the Allies and the prospect of another, more permanent banishment from the civilized world.

She knew she should say something, but she could only stare. This was her chance, and she was as mute as a tree.

"Ahoy, there!" came a shout from over the side of the ship.

"Stay here, miss," the ensign ordered. His motion to the sailors brought two to stand on either side of her as if she were a prisoner like Napoleon. Mayhap he had seen her gaping at Napoleon and feared she would do something out of hand.

The ensign went to where the railing was still open. Peering over it, he shouted, "Keep your distance, you in the jolly boat. This area is restricted to civilians."

"I have come for Miss Dunsworthy!" came back another bellow. "I saw her boat capsize, and I assume you have pulled her out."

Bianca stiffened, then pushed past the men guarding her. They could not stop her, because they were ʿprepared to halt her from getting closer to the emʾⁿeror, not running in the other direction. Stopping by the rail, she waved and called, "Lucian!"

"It would seem," Lucian replied to the ensign as if he had not noticed her on the ship or heard her call his name, "that you have one civilian aboard already."

"She is leaving as soon as our prisoner is transferred to the *Northumberland*."

"Do not be ludicrous. The *Northumberland* has not arrived yet," argued Lucian.

"She cannot leave until our prisoner is transferred."

"Please present my respects to your captain along with my offer to remove Miss Dunsworthy from the *Bellerophon* in this rowboat, so she is not a further impediment to the obvious difficulties of your delicate duties."

Lucian's cool response must have impressed the ensign because he shouted, "Identify yourself."

"Lucian Wandersee, recently a captain in His Royal Highness's service."

Another man pushed through the sailors and stood by the open section of the railing. This man wore the insignia of a lieutenant. "Wandersee? What in the blazes are *you* doing here?"

"Retrieving Miss Dunsworthy at the moment, Blakely." Cupping his hands over his mouth, so his words would not be tossed away by the wind, he called, "Will you grant me permission to board?"

Lieutenant Blakely ordered the rope ladder to be rolled down the side of the boat. "Make sure you tie your jolly boat well to the ladder," he added over the side. He stepped back as Lucian came up on deck. "Welcome aboard, Wandersee. It has been a while."

"Over a year. Our lives have taken a different turn than we expected during our years at Cambridge."

"Yours definitely seems to have." He glanced at Bianca and smiled.

Lucian walked toward her. "Are you ready to go back to shore, Bianca? We should not delay too much longer, for the storm will soon be here."

She looked from Lucian to where the emperor was watching with a hint of a smile on his face. She took one step toward Napoleon. A hand seized her right arm, halting her.

Looking back at the ensign, she said, "I would like to speak to the emp—"

"*General* Bonaparte," the ensign said, emphasizing

the title and earning a fierce frown from Napoleon, "is not receiving visitors, miss."

"But I wish to tell him how many lives he has destroyed with his grasping for an empire."

"General Bonaparte is not receiving visitors, miss."

Lucian interjected, his voice loud enough to carry through the wind to the far side of the deck, as he said in perfect French, "You heard him, Bianca. The *general* is not receiving visitors so you cannot tell him how you have risked your life and your reputation in this effort to send him to St. Helena along with the many ghosts who cannot rest because they fell in the useless battles that won France nothing but destruction."

She struggled not to smile when Lucian winked at her. Raising her own voice, she said in her best French, "I understand he is not receiving visitors so he can never know how we rejoice in the chance we have once again for peace."

The ensign growled a curse, and Lucian put his hand on her left arm.

"I believe, Bianca," Lucian said, switching back to English, "our visit to the *Bellerophon* is at an end." He aimed a glower at the ensign, who quickly lifted his hand off her other arm.

"Thank you," she whispered and bit her lip as Napoleon strode away with his captors in tow. "I never expected *you* would chase after me, Lucian. Not after what we said to each other when we last spoke."

He drew her a step closer. "I do not care if the whole of the British Navy is watching. I want you to know that I was determined that I would not be too late again, Bianca."

"Being too late was what you worried about during your fever."

"Yes."

"What did you fear you would be too late to do?" She bit her lip, tasting salt, before whispering, "I would really like to know if you wish to tell me."

"I wish you to know. I was not worrying about being late to do something, but to meet someone. I was to meet a spy who had information that could halt Napoleon—" His gaze flicked toward the man standing between his guards, then back to her. "I was to meet him, and if I was late, many more men would die. As you can tell, I was not a soldier, exactly."

"What were you exactly?"

"A messenger." His smile was cool. "It was my duty to gather information from those doing reconnaissance and take it to my superiors. The timing of our meetings was always crucial, because the people I met were publicly proponents of Napoleon's government. I always feared I would be too late and put that person in more danger."

"And you were too late?"

"Only once."

She put her fingers to her lips to silence her dismay. Taking her hand, he folded it between his. "Do not look horrified, Bianca. I was not the cause of anyone's death, for I was able to arrange another rendezvous later in the week. However, I knew I must not make such a mistake again. Neither my superiors nor my contacts spoke of that missed meeting, but I had disappointed them, and I would not do so again." He pressed his lips to her hands, and the familiar fire billowed through her, urging her to forget about everything but how she longed to be in his arms. "But my shame at disappointing them was nothing compared to what I have endured since I realized how I have disappointed you. You dared to trust me enough to try to arrange for a marriage between me and Rosie, not knowing that I had no interest in marrying her."

"You did not disappoint me." She took a steadying breath and said, "You broke my heart."

He shook his head. "Impossible!"

"Impossible? I tell you that—"

If she had expected him to argue, she was surprised, for he pulled her to him. As he held her with one arm, he took her chin gently in his fingers and tilted her mouth beneath his. This time, he did not give her a chance to slip away, even if she wanted to. His kiss was as heated as the passions she had seen in his eyes. As his hands curved up her back, she put hers around his shoulders and lost herself in the rapture.

He drew back only far enough to whisper, "Your heart is here." He pressed her fingers over the center of his chest. "Next to mine, which I hope you will accept along with my heartfelt plea that you become my wife, Bianca."

"Your wife?" She was certain she had misunderstood him. Lucian was asking *her* to be his wife?

"I could not imagine marrying Rosie, because I do not love her. I was too busy trying to ignore the truth while in the midst of my attempt to give you a bit of your own matchmaking. The truth is that I love *you*, Bianca. I believe I have since the first moment I saw your lovely face leaning over my sickbed."

"Then why did you try to make a match for me with Mr. Bullock?"

"Because marrying Bianca Dunsworthy frightened me." He laughed as he looked again at Napoleon. "Me, who prided myself in never being afraid to go anywhere in France to do my duty! I was frightened by the thought of entwining my life with yours."

"But you just asked me to be your wife." She could not halt herself from brushing his wind-blown hair back from his eyes.

"Because, even more frightening than entwining my life with yours is the thought of not having you in my life at all. Say you will marry me."

"Yes, I will marry you because I love you, too."

He grinned as he led her toward where Lieutenant Blakely was standing by the open railing. "Your matchmaking and mine seem to have worked very well, although not exactly as we planned."

She smiled up at him as she slipped her fingers through his salt-burnished hair. "Mayhap it was not as we planned, but it is the perfect match."

"For once, sweetheart, we agree, for you will be the perfect bride for me," he whispered before he sealed that promise of a life of happiness with a kiss.

AUTHOR'S NOTE

Look for the next book in the Dunsworthy Brides series *A Primrose Wedding* in July 2005. When Rosie Dunsworthy and her Aunt Millicent join Lord Fortenbury at his country house where his brother is about to be married, Rosie learns her shyness could cost her the very one her heart desires. It would be simpler to conceal that longing in her studies, but will her reading and her music be enough for her when the man of her dreams is being pursued by another very determined woman?

I enjoy hearing from readers. You can contact me at:
Jo Ann Ferguson
PO Box 26
Whitinsville, MA 01588

Check out my web site at:
www.joannferguson.com

Happy reading!

More Regency Romance
From Zebra

More Historical Romance From
Jo Ann Ferguson